FURTHEST
FROM
THE
GATE

Ann Roberts

2007

While threads of reality are woven throughout this book, it is a work of fiction and any resemblance of the characters in this book to people living or dead is purely coincidental—well, some of the time.

Copyright© 2007 by Ann Roberts

Spinsters Ink
P.O. Box 242
Midway, Florida 32343

Printed in the United States of America on acid-free paper
First Edition

Editor: Anna Chinappi
Cover designer: LA Callaghan

ISBN10: 1-883523-81-8
ISBN 13: 978-1-883523-81-7

To my father, a symbol of the many family members who watch their loved ones battle Alzheimer's. May we find a cure quickly, or at the very least, elect politicians who give a damn.

Acknowledgments

I am grateful to many individuals for their support—

Linda Hill for believing in the story
Anna Chinappi for making it better
KS for reading it first
My son for growing into a fine young man with amazing gifts
And Amy, who walks with me through each day, who knows me completely and still loves me—almost as much as I love her.

Author's Note

I would be guilty of plagiarism if I did not acknowledge the contribution made by my uncle, a man whose humor I admired, whose intellect I envied and whose fascination with all people taught me much. Many of the letters included in this novel are of his own wit, while others are my humble attempt to recreate the sound of his voice. My uncle recognized each person for the contribution he or she could make to the human experience, believing that difference is not to be tolerated or accepted—but celebrated.

About the Author

Ann Roberts' first novel *Paid in Full* was published by Bella Books. She lives in Arizona with her family.

Present Day

After one pass through the parking lot, I give up. Normally I wouldn't even bother navigating the roundabout, since the number of spaces seems to equal the number of employees currently on duty at Dayport Care Center. Visitor parking is nonexistent, a testimonial to the reclusive life of the residents, most of whom have been tucked away for their own safekeeping, like valuable family heirlooms placed on display pedestals in a china cabinet.

Today, though, I am in a hurry, trying to sandwich a visit between errands and a stack of essays to grade at home. A close parking spot would have saved me a few minutes. I sigh and park on the street, quickly walking toward the ranch-style brick building, looking at my watch. I haven't even arrived and I am already calculating how long I will stay and when I can leave to maintain my status as a good, dutiful daughter.

A fluorescent pink sign warns KEEP DOOR CLOSED—DOG IN RESIDENCE. I peer through the glass and not seeing Mabel, the ancient, friendly greyhound, I open the door and glance at the nurse on duty. Her eyes meet mine for a second, just long enough to confirm that I am not a wayward homeless person or a deliveryman who might demand her attention.

I work my way through the Great Room, sidestepping haphazardly arranged wheelchairs and walkers, their occupants facing any direction, their intended destinations forgotten. A row of straight-back chairs line the far wall, used by the few residents who are still entirely ambulatory. I wander toward a semicircle of mauve recliners facing a large TV and find my mother lounging in the one closest to the screen, an old movie blaring in Dolby Surround sound. Bing Crosby and Bob Hope travel on the road to somewhere but my mother's gaze, like so many of those around her, is directionless. She stares ahead, her eyes hooded, drugged without drugs. Only when I appear in front of her does she look up, her facial features contorting into an actual expression of happiness, like a camera lens adjusting to the picture frame.

"Hi, Mom," I say with a warm smile.

"Hi there," she replies. Her voice is like sandpaper from lack of use.

I squat down, trying to move closer to her, taking her hand. There are no extra chairs for me and moving to her room would be very troublesome not to mention time consuming. "How are you, Mom? How's your day going?"

This is without a doubt the silliest question I could ask. Her day is no different from yesterday or the day before. She moves from her bed to the recliner, her surroundings changing only when she goes to the dining hall to be fed her meals. Yet I ask the question to continue the charade of hope that her life can be meaningful, even within the walls of this kind and humane prison.

"I'm having some time," she mumbles.

I nod, although I have no idea what she means. All of her words, her entire language, are a code. She speaks English usually, but there is no formal structure, nothing to remind me of her years as a teacher and the time she spent instructing sixth-graders about the placement of nouns and verbs in a sentence. She has become her worst student.

"Charlie was here," she offers.

"Uncle Charlie was visiting? That's great, Mom."

"He said . . . he brought . . ." The sentence evaporates into the air and I cannot make out the end of it. I nod politely, knowing my dead Uncle Charlie couldn't have brought anything except the fond memories my mother carries in her mind.

"Speaking of Uncle Charlie, I have some more of his letters for you to read." I put the copied pages in her lap, well aware that she cannot decipher text and understand paragraphs but hoping she might recognize the handwriting. "I think these were written before I was born, while he was in the Air Force."

"Thank you so much," she gushes. "This is wonderful!"

Her eyes drift away but her hand remains under mine. Bing Crosby is singing now, overpowering the nurses' voices, the ringing phones and the beeping of several monitors. I no longer struggle to create conversation. She is not expecting it. I lean close enough to hear her wheezing, a byproduct of the emphysema that ravages her lungs and permanently tethers her to the oxygen tank next to her.

Not only is she unable to communicate effectively but physically she cannot control any aspect of her movement beyond simple gestures. Like most of the other patients, her skin is the color of paste and deep grooves cross her face from decades of smoking, adding at least fifteen years to her appearance. Only her salt-and-pepper hair signal her true chronological age of sixty-five, the milestone for movie discounts and senior buffet prices, opportunities she will never enjoy.

I stand up again, unable to continue squatting beside her, my own joints feeling middle-aged. The movement gains the attention of several patients whose eyes now stare at me, their faces either full of confusion at the sight of a stranger or happiness because my activity reminds them they are still alive. A thin woman in a pink dress with a mole on her cheek fixates on me, her bland expression unmoving. I smile and get no reaction but she continues to study me since she has nothing but time and I am clearly the most interesting thing in the room.

Their bodies prove that individuality evaporates with age—their stooped shoulders curve into a question mark, the small tufts of gray and white hair that remain on their heads, the plainness of their clothes designed for easy access to their bowels and bodies and most of all, their expressions, which are carbon copies with only a few variations. Their mouths hang open slightly whether they are asleep or awake and their eyes are vacant, all the glimmer and excitement having vanished with age, disease or both. It is difficult to tell whether some are alive or dead, only the slight rise and fall of their chests keeping the doctors from signing the death certificates.

I look at my mother, robbed of her uniqueness, the very soul of her essence and the memories that defined her. She is no different than anyone else here. The pages of everyone's journal have been erased, leaving only small random paragraphs to tell their stories and the outer shells to wither and decay in this room. Their minds cling to what little is left, the most vivid imprints that remain.

Signs of life surround the residents, the sleeping greyhound in the corner, the parakeets singing in the nearby cage and the endless kinetic motion of the nurses' station. Even the bright blue walls give the residents a reason to force their hearts to beat a little longer, for in such a vibrant environment the desire for life is strong. At least that must be what the Dayport Care Center trustees believe.

I lean against the nearby wall, scanning the faces, the rows of people waiting. Their walkers and wheelchairs form a gauntlet at this finish line.

Waiting to die.

Waiting to arrive at the Pearly Gates and see Saint Peter. They could use this sunset to ponder their existence and their imminent death, yet their decrepit minds prevent such thoughts, and maybe that is the Great Architect's plan, a sign of compassion for these fragile beings who wander through the final chapter of the book of their lives.

I glance about again, recognizing that collectively they have lived over two thousand years, their existence marked by the joy they brought, the tragedy they created, the despair they endured.

Whose pages will be most impressive and earn a place at the front of Saint Peter's gate?

The hands of the large wall clock have descended deeper into the hour and I realize I have been with my mother for nearly twenty minutes. My allocated time allotment is half an hour but if I leave early, only I will know. She will make no guilty swipes at my conscience as she did in my youth, none of the care workers will shake their heads disapprovingly and my father will never ask how long I stayed with my mother. Remembering two other things that loom on my agenda for the day, I pat her on the arm and lean down once more.

"Mom, I'm going to need to go. I've got some more errands to do. I'll come by tomorrow and see you."

"Hmm," she says. "Well, I'm not sure if I'll be around. I've got a luncheon with the governor and then three meetings back to back. You may not see me," she adds with a doubtful tone.

A smile crosses my face. "That's okay, Mom. I'll find you. You don't worry, because I'll find you."

May 20, 1963

Dear Sister Mine,

I have deduced what was obvious to everyone else in my life: I am entirely unsuited for military service. Considering I've now been at Fort Whitlock for one week, I feel I can fairly assess my aptitude for defending our nation and the positions for which I am qualified. They include, in no particular order, Official B-2 Bomber Window Washer, Stamp Licker to the General Attaché, or Court Jester.

My superior officer, Lieutenant Wyrick, would say that I'm overqualified for the latter position. In fact my antics may be chiefly responsible for his impending heart attack or the U.S.'s deteriorating relationship with Cuba.

Just yesterday we had a surprise locker inspection. Since I was relatively certain my locker would not pass muster, and I didn't think the good lieutenant would notice I was missing, I contortioned myself inside the locker and peeked out the vent slits. I quickly realized my ruse would soon be discovered, as protocol required all new recruits to stand at the foot of their beds during the inspection. Even dimwitted Lieutenant Wyrick keenly observed that Private Charles Driscoll's bed had no one at its helm.

"Where's Driscoll?" Wyrick bellowed at poor Airman Johnson, the unfortunate lad who bunks next to me and endures my late night penury and constant snoring.

"I DON'T KNOW, SIR!" he squawked, his post-pubescent voice cracking at the end.

Wyrick turned and faced the locker, his pencil-thin mustache in stark contrast to his chalk-white face. He sported a freshly buzzed flattop and I could see his gritted teeth from my vantage point.

He stared down at my poorly made cot and his eyes settled on the locker. I watched him advance toward me, the click of his heels echoing throughout the silent barracks, his individual short hairs becoming more distinct with each step.

I smiled as the latch turned and the door flung open. I said the only thing that came to mind: "Going up?"

Lieutenant Wyrick, as you might imagine, was not amused. And if you've ever wondered if all of those sophomoric punishments you see in the movies are really employed by military personnel, such as cleaning the latrine with your toothbrush—they are. Can you send me a quarter for a new toothbrush?

As for Christmas, no gift is necessary. Your announcement of the "Blessed Event" was met with much elation. I am thrilled for you and Joe. As I have told our mother, I consider myself perfectly suited for the role of an uncle. I am really not too concerned over the child's sex (so long as you agree it should have one) nor am I unduly worried about its horoscope. Also, I do approve of your choice of names. Kate is a strong name and reminds me of Katharine Hepburn, while Henry would be equally appropriate, should the Y chromosome prove dominant. I trust you and Joe will adjust to being parents. As for your inevitable discomfort, I only give a slight bit of sympathy. I told you what would happen if you got married. You are a good Catholic with bad rhythm.

Joe, you must be patient with my sister. Once, in a rare moment of sibling magnanimity, I tried to explain to her the biological aspects of marriage but she just mumbled something about there being nothing disturbing about storks.

I will be sending you a Christmas present, dear sister. I'm knitting you a brassiere. Right now I'm working on the left cup and would like you to cooperate by putting on a little weight on your left side only.

I must go. Lieutenant Wyrick will return shortly and I'm supposed to be guarding this chain-link fence from the barbarians of lower Ohio who will inevitably storm the gate. Again, I proclaim my happiness at your good news, which can only be surpassed by your own joy. The population problem be damned! Take care and don't worry. The chances are a thousand to one that the little son of a gun will ever resemble me—let alone think like me.

Mazeltov!
Charles

August 8, 1967

Dearest Sister Mine:

I'm sorry I can't remember much about my last letter. That particular evening I had rinsed my cerebellum in septic pools of Schotch (damn typewriter) and I find it very difficult even recalling the fact that I wrote you a letter. However, in the clear light of sobriety, I state my congratulations to you on the adoption of your second child. I think Thomas is an outstanding name. Hopefully, he won't be doubtful. I know you have to wait a long time for him to come home with you but it will be well worth it.

The evening I penned my last letter did not end with the licking of an envelope. No indeed! With wild abandon, I led a raucous mob of two other airmen upon the semi-civilized populace of Cleveland, where we waged a furious battle against Demon Rum. We lost, largely by virtue of insincerity. One of my comrades, Dirk Moore, became a trifle overzealous in his efforts to strike a blow for Democracy and passed out while charging up the steps of the Cleveland City Hall, intending to liberate the hundreds of political prisoners he was certain were suffering within. It was an hour before we could awaken him and from there we journeyed to another local pub and led the many customers in a community sing. What transpired after that point is known only by the several frightened old ladies whose lives we lengthened by making flirtatious suggestions to.

I am pleased to write that I ran into my old friend Nestor. He drove up on the day of my discharge and we trekked out to Santa Barbara. We drank enough Budweiser to justify a stock split and then went looking for our mutual friend Jim. We brought a bucket of beer as an offering and Jim was pleased. Jim, an anthropologist, was angered when Nestor suggested that primitive man first gathered together in order to grow grain so they could make beer. I didn't take part in the debate, for I was lusting after Jim's wife. I tried to convince her that only the Eskimos really know how to treat their guests. The host always gives his friends the best food, lodging, beer and even throws in his wife for good measure. She wouldn't have anything to do with it but I partook in much good food and beer. Jim eventually passed out (beer does that) and Nestor and I spent the night on the floor. I was sorry to see Nestor leave, but we both ran out of cash (beer does that, too).

You asked me what I'll do, now that I'm free of the Air Force. Who knows? I may join the Peace Corps. I may join the Viet Cong. I may go back to college. I may take up beachcombing. Will I reenlist? Will the Pope be circumcised? Regardless of what I do, I will probably continue to love hating it. That's the way I am, or haven't you noticed?

Your rather honorably discharged brother,
Charles

Not Your Typical Girl

Top row—fourth from the left. That's where Kimmie Lancaster stood for our first grade picture. She was easy to spot, the only girl amidst the tall six-year-old boys. A young Helen of Troy, she towered over the rest of us in stature and beauty. She wasn't very bright, so we were never in the same skills groups but I always found an excuse to pass her desk during the day. My pencil was dull or my bladder was full, anything just to glance at that porcelain face.

I always avoided any meaningful contact. We never played together or sat next to each other on the bus. I watched from afar as Kimmie's best friends touched her shimmering blonde hair, wrapped their arms around her slight frame and best of all, kissed her perfect lips, which always seemed to form a pout. I marveled at how easy it was for Heather Bowens to take Kimmie's hand, something I wouldn't dare do. Every time I looked at Kimmie I felt sick, sick in the most wonderful of ways. My stomach plunged like a runaway elevator and my tongue expanded, making only guttural sounds possible. How did Heather do it? Didn't she just want to spend hours looking at Kimmie?

I'd been so distracted watching Kimmie make o's during penmanship (her mouth kept forming the letter as she wrote) that I'd been scolded by Mrs. Locke. "Kate Mitchell, keep your eyes on your paper, young lady. Class, remember, letter formation is critical to good writing."

I lived for lunchtime. Mrs. Locke would put the boys and girls in two lines alphabetically and I got to stand right behind Kimmie, within inches of that honey scented hair and those magnificent lips.

Before we'd begin our march to the cafeteria, Mrs. Locke would turn toward us and flash two perfect rows of dentures. "Now ladies, look at the little boy across from you. Maybe someday that will be the man you marry."

I glanced at Ralph Needleman, his hair plastered to his head with Dippity-Do. I couldn't imagine any girl talking to him, let alone marrying him. Everyone knew he had cooties. No, if I had to get married, I'd marry Kimmie. There was only one problem.

She was standing in the wrong line.

My father's car pulled into the driveway and I heard the familiar sounds of his entrance. Seeing my mother on the phone, he kissed me on the head. "Hey."

"Hi, Daddy! How was work?" I asked, trying to sound like my mother.

My father looked at me seriously. "You wouldn't know anything about construction code violations, would you?"

I shook my head. I knew my father was a civil engineer but I had no idea what that meant. "I'm only in first grade, Daddy. Maybe we'll get to that next year."

He nodded and smiled. "You just might."

We looked at my mother, the epitome of Betty Crocker, stirring the vegetables with one hand, cigarette in the other, watching my young siblings Tommy and Karen play on the floor. "I think this committee could be very important, Estelle. The superintendent of schools wants to actively involve all of the PTAs in the district and mobilize them. He's

very concerned about declining enrollment. I need you to serve with me."
My mother listened to Estelle's obvious hesitation, already shaking her
head. "Just think about it, okay? All right, I'll talk to you tomorrow."

She hung up and smiled at my father. "Hi, honey." They exchanged
their customary evening kiss and retreated to the bedroom for adult
decompression time, as my father called it.

"What's adult decompression?" I'd once asked him.

"A time just for adults to talk," he said. "In other words, it's all about
boring stuff."

"Oh, so I'm not missing anything really important," I concluded.

"Not at all. Whenever the topic of Christmas toys, Disneyland or the
president comes up, you're there," he assured me.

Dinner was always at 6 o'clock. We sat down and said grace and then
talked about our very different days while my mother fed my infant sister
and my father oversaw my three-year-old brother's messy eating habits.

"How was school?" my father started.

I frowned. "Mrs. Locke says that I can't wear my six-shooters or my
cowboy hat anymore."

His eyes narrowed. "Why not?"

"Because," my mother interjected, "the guns are a distraction to
the other students and the cowboy hat isn't ladylike enough." My
father opened his mouth but my mother quickly cut him off. "I'm just
paraphrasing, dear."

"Hmm," my father thought. "Well, I understand about the pistols
but unless there's a rule about hats at school, Katie, you can wear that hat
any day you want."

My mother shook her head in disagreement. "Joe, Katie would benefit
from some ladylike manners."

"I don't care about being a lady!" I exclaimed.

"Well, dear, someday you might," my mother said.

"She'll have plenty of time to be a lady," my father responded. "And
wear high heels, and all that other stuff." He looked at me and winked
before turning back to my mother. "Besides, Barbara, where's your sense
of individuality? The ACLU would revoke your membership if they
heard that talk."

My mother busied herself with my little brother's vegetables and ignored my father. "Katie, I don't have any problem with your jeans and T-shirts but every once in a while it would be nice if you wore one of the lovely pinafores grandma made you."

I shook my head violently. "No, no, no!"

Realizing the conversation would go nowhere, my father changed the subject. "Did you see Nixon's press conference on TV today?"

My mother pursed her lips and passed me the meat. "There's something about that man that I just don't trust. I can't put my finger on it but he just doesn't seem honest."

"Nixon, Nixon, he's our man, McGovern belongs in the garbage can!" I sang.

My father and mother both stared at me. "Why would you want to put Senator McGovern in a garbage can?" my father asked.

I really had no idea. It was just how the song went. I shrugged my shoulders.

"Do you know what Mr. McGovern stands for, Katie?" My mother looked at me with questioning eyes. "He's done many good things for people and he favors removing the troops from Vietnam."

I knew all about Vietnam and the soldiers who were dying. "Well, maybe he shouldn't be in a garbage can," I said.

My father stared at me. "Kate, I've got one word I want you to learn. Democrat."

"Democrat," I repeated.

"Good," my father said with another wink.

My mother wiped goulash from my brother's mouth and turned to me. "Katie, honey, I do have something I need to speak with you about. It's very exciting!"

"Is it a pony? Are we getting a pony!"

"No," my father added.

"No, honey, it's not a pony. One of my old students is getting married and she would like you to be the flower girl. Isn't that wonderful?" Her face became overly animated and I sensed something was up.

"What do I have to do?" I asked suspiciously.

"You just walk down the aisle ahead of the bride and drop flower petals. Simple." I noticed my mother glanced at my father, who quickly studied his dinner.

"Sounds stupid to me," I grunted.

My mother noticed my sour expression. "It's a very important job, Kate. And I think it's extremely nice of Lucille to think of you—and me. She said I was her favorite teacher."

"Mom, I don't even know her," I protested.

"But I do. Besides, Robby Wentworth's going to be the ring-bearer, so you'll have a friend to talk to."

The last thing I wanted to do was talk to Robby Wentworth, my only sometimes friend.

My mother stared at me, waiting for an answer. The right answer.

"Mom, I don't want to," I whined.

She sighed. "Well, I'm not going to force you." She rose from the table and began collecting the dinner dishes.

Years ago my mother had perfected the art of Anger with Dishware. Plates crashed against each other and glasses smacked, just approaching breakage but staying intact. She had resorted to the lowest of blows— unspoken Catholic guilt.

I crumbled. "Okay."

Mom set down the plates and hugged me. "Oh, and by the way, your dress fitting's tomorrow."

"Dress? I have to wear a dress?" My father grabbed the remaining innocent dishes and headed for the kitchen.

Mom laughed nervously. "Of course you'll wear a dress. This is a wedding! You can't wear your cruddy old jeans."

"I'm not wearing a dress!"

"Kate Elizabeth Mitchell, you will be in that wedding, and you will wear a dress, or you won't play basketball for a month."

"Fine!" I screamed. I ran to my room and threw myself onto the bed, punching my pillow several times.

The doorknob clicked as she entered the room. My left eyeball focused on her slight frame, the blonde bobbed hair and the hands that perpetually rested in the pockets of her house dress.

"Katie, let's compromise. Look at me, please."

I turned around, my head still against the pillow.

My mother's face softened. "If you'll be in the wedding, I'll get you a new backboard. Is that fair?"

I nodded. At the time it seemed like a victory. I was wrong.

Lucille Orcutt was a battalion commander draped in lace and satin. She personally oversaw all the wedding preparations inside the cramped dressing room of Our Lady of the Valley Church. A bow was not tied, a bang was not curled and a cheek was not rouged without Lucille's approval. She had just checked my hair ribbon for the third time before darting over to a bridesmaid with a slipper problem.

I slumped into a chair. Across the room I saw my reflection in a full-length mirror. I looked like a piece of mold. My pea-green dress supposedly provided contrast to the emerald green worn by the bridesmaids. The floor length gown was too long and I couldn't see the black patent leather shoes that suffocated my tiny feet. My long, brown hair had been pulled back and tied with a matching pea-green bow. A piece of mold with a tail.

I closed my eyes as I drove to the hoop for a layup, the basketball bouncing off my new backboard and then, swish! Two points. Actually the backboard was currently sitting in the garage, purchased three days before the wedding. Although my parents had never reneged on a promise before, it couldn't hurt to be safe.

Lucille dashed over and pulled me to my feet. "Now cutie, let me give you the once over." While she examined me, I reached my own conclusions. Her future husband must have been drunk or in a poorly lit room when he proposed. Lucille's face was all forehead, her dime-sized eyes, pig nose and button mouth sat somewhere near her chin. I did a better job putting a face on Mr. Potatohead.

Her neck smiled. "You're all set." She adjusted my bow and squeezed my cheeks. "You are so cute!" Before I could stamp on her foot, she was gone.

After what seemed like twenty years, we all lined up. I stood behind Robby, holding my basket of flower petals. My job was easy. I walked down the aisle and *gently* tossed the petals from side to side. The gently part had been emphasized by my mother, Lucille and the wedding hostess at least ten times.

"So what do you do?" I asked Robby. He'd been ignoring me but he turned around when I addressed him.

"I carry this little pillow to the front."

"Why?"

"So everybody can see the rings." He held out an enormous burgundy pillow. In the center sat two rings secured to the velvet by white ribbons.

It occurred to me Robby's job was even easier. All he had to do was carry the pillow. I had the immense responsibility of carrying the basket *and* tossing the petals. What if I screwed up? What if the petals all stuck together? What if I didn't toss them correctly?

"Robby, why don't we switch?" I offered. "You drop the petals and I'll carry the rings."

Robby rolled his eyes at me. "I can't carry the flowers. There's no such thing as a flower *boy*. Everybody'd think I was a sissy."

My face clouded and Robby's mouth clamped shut.

"Are you calling me a sissy?" My hand tightened around the basket handle. The wedding hostess appeared and Robby whirled around, hoping to end our confrontation.

The church doors opened and strains of *Ode to Joy* echoed through the room. The first set of smiling attendants advanced toward the altar and our procession inched forward. My basket of flowers bumped Robby's butt and he spun around, thinking I was provoking him again.

"Stop doing that!" he spat. We took two more steps, and I did it again—this time on purpose.

"Katie, I'm warning you."

"You called me a sissy."

"Well, you are!"

Before I could whack him in the rump again, the two of us were standing in front of the open doors, facing the three hundred guests. I was hot. My tossing hand clenched some defenseless posies and I threw them in the air. Instead of landing on the ground, they flew up into Robby's face.

"Stop it," he hissed.

"I will not," I said, showering him with another handful of flowers.

Robby stopped walking. "Goddammit, Katie, you're gonna get it!" The little velvet pillow crashed down on my head. As he readied for a second blow, I smashed him broadside with the basket. An explosion of petals filled the aisle.

Although the guests were horrified, no one did anything. The organist played (her view obstructed by the mighty Wurlitzer), the groom laughed, the preacher thumbed through his Bible and those guests nearest to us merely wiped the posies and daisies from their clothes. Robby and I continued whacking each other and yelling obscenities until a scream pierced the air. Lucille Orcutt chugged down the aisle, brandishing her bouquet like a bayonet. She was a huge snowball rolling toward us. Robby and I did what all children would do—we ran. Robby scooted behind the best man and I hustled onto the altar next to the maid of honor.

In my hurry I forgot about the tall step that we had all been warned about during rehearsal. My foot, caught in the folds of the dress, hit the step and I tumbled over it. The basket rolled into a corner and the dress flew over my head, exposing my clean, white underpants to the entire company.

I sat upright. A ripple of laughter began with the groomsmen and quickly overtook the bridesmaids. It spread through the string quartet and soon engulfed the audience. The only people not laughing were the mothers of the bride and groom, Lucille and my mother. Lucille had to be restrained by the preacher. Luckily he was stronger than he looked.

Once the rings were found and the groom recovered from an awful case of hiccups, Lucille Orcutt became Lucille Widentower.

At the reception Lucille carefully avoided me and my parents but many of the guests came by and shook my hand. Some just laughed and one man slipped me five dollars and told me I was the only good thing about the whole day. I'm not sure, but I think he was Lucille's father.

The drive home was solemn. My mother stared at the windshield, never looking at me and refusing to acknowledge my father's pathetic attempts at conversation with more than a grunt. I knew she'd eventually say something while I was a captive in a moving car.

As we pulled into the driveway, I readied my hand on the door latch, preparing for a quick exit the second my father got the car into park. Before I could escape, though, my mother swiftly turned and popped the door lock into place.

"I have never been so humiliated in my whole life. That was the most insensitive thing you have ever done, Kate Mitchell."

"Robby started it!" I blurted.

"Young lady, that is not the point. You embarrassed all of us and you ruined Lucille's wedding. A girl only gets married once."

"Well, I'm never getting married!"

"And you can kiss that backboard good-bye."

My mother stormed out of the car before I could protest. I sat there, picking at some old gum from the door handle and waiting for my father's wrath, since parental abuse usually comes consecutively. I waited but he just sat there.

My attention wandered to the gum, which was becoming exceedingly resistant to my finger. My father made a noise. It sounded like a belch but I couldn't tell. We sat there a while longer and then he did it again. By the fourth time I realized it wasn't a belch but a giggle. Unable to contain himself any longer, he belly laughed and pounded the steering wheel with both hands. He even honked the horn. He looked at me, tears rolling down his face, and I laughed too. I laughed until my stomach hurt and by then I'd crawled over the front seat and into my father's wide arms.

We sat there until we could breathe again, enjoying the moment. It wasn't very often that my father got to be the good parent while my mother played the heavy. Usually the roles were reversed and my father seemed to savor the change.

Only after we'd given mom a good half hour to cool off, did we go inside. Once I'd apologized to her, written a letter of apology to Lucille and said one hundred Hail Mary's for swearing in church, my father and I put up the backboard and played ball until dark.

October 15, 1970

My dearest Katie,

Thank you for that wonderful letter. On the very day that it arrived, I had been talking with two of my friends about you and your family. We had been talking about people we liked a lot and you guys were about the only ones I could think of. My friends' names are Merle and Peebee. They live, and you're not going to believe this, in the storm drains underneath the city of Tucson. This is not a lie. Merle and PeeBee actually live down there. Both of them are eighteen and they make money by selling little trinkets that they make in the storm drain. Of course, when it rains, they have a hard time but they manage. They grab their trinkets and run like all beejeezus.

Now, your parents are going to try to tell you that I am making this up. It is not so. Merle and Peebee really do exist and they do live in the storm drain. I showed them your letter and they thought that it was one of the most beautiful things written.

Merle and Peebee wouldn't lie.

My dear Katie, it is the duty of we grown-ups to encourage you kids to do certain things and not to do other things. Well, here is my two cents worth.

If you can love your family as much as your family loves you, then you will have no problems at all. Ever.

Love,

Your Uncle Charlie

Present Day

Today she is talkative and active. She holds the remote control to her lounger, the connecting wire firmly grasped in her hands, much the way a woman would hold her purse on a bus. It is tangled and knotted in places, and her fingers flex up and down as she works to straighten the cord but her mind is unable to process the steps of the operation. Nothing is accomplished except new configurations of the same knots.

"What is that you have in your hand, Mom?" I point to the remote's cord and touch it.

"Oh, this . . . this . . . this . . . is Aquinas."

"Aquinas?"

"Yes."

"I see."

"I've been trying . . . but and comes . . . did you bring the little girl? It's not farblung . . ."

I listen as the switches in her mind turn on and off, sometimes allowing her access to the language that was so dear to her, but more often denying her the right of coherence. She speaks in a foreign tongue for several more minutes and I can only make out shadows of words that she can't quite remember.

When her mouth finally goes still, I speak. "Mom, I've got some bad news. Do you remember Cousin Margaret?"

"Yes."

"Mom, she died yesterday."

"Oh, no!" My mother's reaction to this unfortunate news is the clearest I've seen in weeks. Margaret is my mother's second cousin and her last living relative. She was eighty-nine and lived in the room next to my mother at the care center.

"She was really tired, Mom. She couldn't breathe anymore and she just went to sleep."

"I . . . she . . ."

"Mom, we're trying to contact the other people who are getting part of the inheritance with you. Do you remember Thelda?"

"Uh-huh."

"Who was she?"

"John and her mom knew each other at . . . at . . ."

"The orphanage?"

"Yes. She was almost a sister to him. The same people took them both in."

John is Margaret's deceased husband and since my father is only related to these people by marriage, his knowledge of the family connections is foggy. It is my mother who has this information in the vault of her mind and it pains me to realize how much other family history will dissolve with her memory loss.

"That's who I thought she was. Mom, what about a woman named Frankie?"

"Oh, Frankie owned the rarie. John knew her."

"What did you say, Mom?"

"Frankie owned the rarie with John."

"But Frankie and Thelda weren't related, right?"

She shakes her head and says, "No," emphatically.

I have no idea what a *rarie* is and I doubt John ever owned one but the mystery of Frankie will need to be investigated by the expensive attorneys hired to probate Margaret's will. The cost to find the other mysterious beneficiary will be phenomenal and cut into the inheritance, money that could be used for my mother's care, but there is no other way since I cannot access the necessary information and have clearly exhausted my mother's long-term memory.

"I'm so sorry about Margaret," she says again.

"I know Mom, but it was her time." I think back to the night before, my father and I standing over Margaret's hospital bed, as she used every bit of energy to take each single breath, her mouth wide open, unaware of our presence while the thread of life disappeared. I imagine my mother's death will be just as cruel and inhumane.

An aide dressed in blue scrubs comes by and leans over my mother, a genuine smile on her face. "Hi, Barbara! How are you today?"

"I'm fine," my mother responds, her face full of animation. "How are you today, Carol?"

"I'm great," the woman said. I notice her name tag reads "Beverly," but she doesn't seem to mind being Carol. "We're about ready for lunch, so let's get you going."

I move out of the way and watch Beverly shift my mother from the lounger into her wheelchair, almost effortlessly. I shake my head, remembering the many times my brother and I had dropped my mother, trying to move her from the wheelchair to the toilet seat or to the bed. Beverly clearly knows what she's doing.

My mother chats with "Carol" all the way to the dining hall, asking her about family she may or may not have. It's obvious my mother has not lost her ability to charm others. I remember her slogan from her days of campaigning for a legislative seat. "Barbara Mitchell: The People Person." I am comforted to see a sliver of her old self.

"Would you like to stay and feed her?" Beverly asks.

I'm somewhat anxious but I agree, partially because to say no would be unsupportive and while I want to help my mother as much as I can, having to feed a woman with a master degree and a near genius IQ revolts me. I cannot explain any of this to Beverly, so I smile and maneuver my mother to her customary spot at the small, square table.

My mother is seated with two other women who also need assistance.

Lunch consists of pot roast, mashed potatoes and carrots. The precut piece of beef looks decent and the potatoes are genuine and not powdered. My mother has no reaction to the lunchtime selections or her tablemates. Her inability to make conversation or at least acknowledge those around her would offend her Midwestern sensibilities, if she remembered she had any. Periodically my mother reaches for the fork I hold, a feeble gesture since her hand shakes as it touches mine.

"It's okay, Mom. I've got it," I say, trying to keep the potatoes from falling into my lap. She chews everything slowly, not so much to savor the flavor of each bite but because she forgets what she's doing. I glance around at those feeding themselves. A few struggle to keep the food on their utensils and I know they will soon be joining my mother at this table.

Many are slow but capable. I wonder what cataclysmic moment compelled a loved one to finally pick up the phone and contact a facility or a caseworker. Most likely procrastination prevailed and the call only came when the proverbial camel had broken his back—or a family member had sustained an equally serious injury. For my family it had been my father breaking his ribs when he tried to lift my mother off the toilet seat by himself, and they both crashed against the side of the tub, thus proving seventy-five-year-old men should not lift heavy objects, even if it is the object of their entire affection.

As I raise the fork to her lips again, I see that her head is cocked toward her left shoulder, her mouth wide open. She has fallen asleep and is snoring quietly. I set the fork down and motion to the nurse that I will be leaving. I do not wake her, violating one of the cardinal rules of our home. No one ever left our house without saying good-bye, since life was so fragile and unpredictable. As a teenager, I was always required to find her and tell her I was going out, even if it meant rousing her from a deserved nap. Although I let her sleep now, I still do my part and kiss her good-bye, forgiving her for not returning the gesture.

The Birds and the Bees

In the 1970s, Phoenix was a town, not a city. A drive down any major road yielded as many lettuce patches as housing developments. The developers were only beginning to see the value of the area's pleasant weather and flat land, easy landscape on which to build. Phoenix's downtown was the size of a postage stamp and the surrounding residential housing branched out only a few miles in any direction. Most everyone was from somewhere else and the rest of the country surmised new settlers arrived by covered wagon, rather than station wagon.

They came to Arizona with many of their myths and fallacies about the Southwest intact. These new transplants, like many other Americans, believed all Arizonans rode on horseback, attempting to scalp marauding Indians while spouting the ultraconservative views of Senator Barry Goldwater. Disputes were settled at high noon in front of the large saguaro cactus, the only plant believed to grow in Arizona. On weekends the entire state journeyed on horseback to see our Natural Wonder of the

World, the Grand Canyon. In actuality Arizona had shed its Wild West image long ago, and the only people wearing ten-gallon hats and chaps were the visiting tourists from Iowa.

The greatest taboo of all was sex. Children in Arizona were taught that babies came from that evil, liberal, godless state to the West—California. So of course, no one in Arizona had sex. End of discussion. I suspected there was more and during the summer after second grade, I enticed my former nemesis turned best friend, Robby Wentworth, to play a new game called *Doctor,* which I'd heard about from my friend, Denise (yes, she was from California).

We waited until my mother was engrossed in her afternoon soap operas before tip-toeing up the stairs and quietly shutting the door to my parents' bathroom. We were both nervous, only Robby wouldn't admit it because he was a boy. He tried to look cool by folding his arms across his chest and it would have been believable, except his knocking knees reverberated in the small bathroom.

"You go first," he squeaked.

I sighed. "Okay." I wiggled out of my white shorts and peeled off my underwear, revealing my undeveloped nether regions. Robby stared at my crotch. His eyes widened and his arms fell limp. He looked like an abandoned marionette.

"Well?" I asked impatiently.

The marionette came to life and inched toward me. Standing nose to nose I could smell the garlic on his breath from lunch. He tried to bend down, but the bathroom was so small that he couldn't position himself between my legs. He attempted several angles, but each time his feet were crushed against the baseboard, or his head bumped the toilet.

"This isn't working," he growled.

"What if I stood up here?" I suggested. I lowered the toilet seat and stepped up, while Robby parted my thighs and his face disappeared. All I could see was the bald crown of his head, the place where Leonard Grossmeir had stuck a wad of gum the previous week.

My eyes drifted to the row of ducklings walking across the shower curtain. The whole bathroom was ducks and geese, including the towels, the rug and the trash can. Even the soap dish was shaped like a mallard. Amidst this shrine to waterfowl hung my father's old brown towel. He said the idea of rubbing a duck over his body made him sick.

I tried not to think of Robby stuck there between my legs, seeing my most private of parts, places that even I hadn't seen. I'd tried several times to look at myself with a mirror, but I couldn't get my hand, my legs and my eyes in the right place at the same time. All I'd managed to see was the lint on the underside of my belly button.

"Now that's kinda different." Robby's face reappeared and he stared up at me.

"What'd you see?"

"Well there really wasn't that much to look at. Just some pink skin."

"It's my turn," I said quickly, very curious to see what Robby had hidden in his pants.

I jumped off the toilet so Robby could take my place. Instead of eagerly complying, he recoiled into the corner of the bathroom.

"I need to go home now," he whimpered.

"Liar!" I yelled. I pounced on him, pummeling his arms and shoulders with my clenched fists. He tried to stand, but realizing it was hopeless, he shrank into a tight little ball. "Robby Wentworth, you're a welcher! We made a deal."

Slowly Robby rose from the floor, his body pressed against the wall. He fumbled with his belt buckle, unzipped his pants and dropped them to the floor. At the sight of his Snoopy and Woodstock boxers, I giggled.

"What's so funny?" he snapped. "At least my momma don't pick out my undies."

He had a point. My mother was an underwear freak. She believed little girls should wear all-white, cotton briefs. No colors, no designs and no stains. Her theory was that children would inevitably wind up in the emergency room and she'd be damned if her child would be caught in dirty, old, flowered skivvies.

"Well, take 'em off," I commanded.

Robby's eyes studied the tile. "I don't want to."

Without warning, I yanked his boxers down—and blinked. Robby's pee-pee hung there like a limp noodle. I didn't know what to make of it. Maybe Robby was defective. I stared at it and Robby flinched, his hands covering his crotch.

"C'mon, Robby, let me see it! You promised."

Robby slowly put his hands by his side. He really wasn't that much to look at. In fact I thought his penis was ugly and it reminded me of a piece of sausage. I tried to imagine what it would be like to wear sausage between my legs all the time. It sounded uncomfortable and I suddenly felt very fortunate to be a girl.

"Do you want to touch it, Katie?"

"No!" I exclaimed. "Why would I want to touch it?"

"My Uncle Frank touches it."

I blinked. "He does? Why would your Uncle Frank touch your pee-pee?"

Robby shrugged his shoulders. "I don't know. He just did it and told me not to tell anyone. He told me if I kept quiet, he'd give me a dollar every time I let him touch it. I got thirty dollars now," he said proudly.

"That's a lot of money," I said, hoisting myself onto the vanity. "I wish I had an Uncle Frank." I swung my legs back and forth, suddenly bored with the Doctor game.

My mother's voice suddenly rose above the whir of the fan. "Katie? Are you in there?" she said as she opened the door. When she saw Robby and I, both naked from the waist down, her mouth fell open. She quickly recovered and took a deep breath.

"Robby, I think you should put your clothes on now and go home. Katie, will you please get dressed and join me downstairs?"

She left and Robby and I looked at each other, terrified. "Do you think she'll tell my mom?" Robbie gasped as he put on his boxers.

I shook my head. "I don't know. She didn't look that mad."

We quickly pulled on our shorts and headed down the stairs. Robby shot out of the front door like a bullet, a loud good-bye lost in the slam that came after his exit.

I found my mother sitting on the couch, a book opened in her lap. I joined her and she patted my knee.

"Katie, can you tell me what you and Robby were doing in the bathroom?" she asked gently, still smiling.

A rush of relief swept over me. I wasn't going to die. "We were just looking at each other," I said truthfully.

My mother nodded, and she seemed relieved as well. "That's

understandable. You're at that age now where you're beginning to realize that boys and girls are different. Is that what you discovered today? That your body is different from Robby's body?"

I just nodded, not wanting to tell my mother how disgusting Robby's body really was. I figured my father must have a larger version of Robby and my mother must have found something attractive about it.

She pointed to the book, which she had opened to two diagrams facing each other. On the left side was the picture of a naked man, several arrows pointing to various parts of his body. On the right side was the picture of a woman, who was also covered with arrows. "Men and women are different, Katie, for a reason. It has to do with reproduction, the way human beings make babies."

Oh, I thought. Babies. I already knew this thanks to Denise's older sister. She'd told us all about sex and getting pregnant. It had something to do with jacks and balls. So I just thought I'd never play that game and I would never have to worry.

My mother discussed the parts of the male and I couldn't explain why, but I didn't like looking at the male body. The male was much more angular, with square shoulders and a broad chest. The expression on his hairy face was serious and unfriendly and I envisioned him crushing objects between his powerful hands. Eventually my mother began explaining how the penis worked and I realized her version of this story was a little different than the one I'd heard from Denise.

"You mean it can get bigger?" I was flabbergasted.

"Yes. When a male is excited, his penis will harden and get longer."

I was repulsed. It was bad enough that guys had to wear a sausage but to think that it could grow was really sickening. How uncomfortable.

I politely listened to the rest of my mother's explanation about the human male but my eyes had already wandered to the female figure. There was nothing that appealed to me about the male figure, especially now that I knew about the penis. If I developed a prejudice against the male body, it really was the fault of *Gray's Anatomy.*

I paid close attention as my mother explained the difference between men and women and it was clear to me that the female body was much more advanced and certainly more desirable.

Everything about a woman seemed smooth and careful, like a winding road whose gentle curves were natural and comforting. I was fascinated by the slope of the woman's shoulders, amazed at the way each part of the body cascaded into the next. I followed the outline of the figure, noting the small waist and expansive hips. Most fascinating, though, were the woman's breasts and it was there that my eyes remained riveted for the rest of the conversation.

Eventually my mother hit upon the topic of nursing a baby, but I wasn't paying attention. "Will my breasts grow? I mean for sure?" I interrupted.

"Of course, Katie. As you get into seventh or eighth grade your breasts will grow as you turn into a woman. Now I think I've given you enough information for today." She closed the book and placed it back on the shelf. "I know that you will have questions about all of this and I want you to come to me and ask me anything. Okay?" I nodded and she smiled. "I don't, however, think it's a good idea for you and Robby to take your clothes off in front of each other anymore. Can we not do that again?"

"Uh-huh," I agreed.

Reassured that I would no longer engage in exhibitionism, she went back to the kitchen and resumed her multitude of phone calls to her school committee members. I went to the book shelf and removed the anatomy book, immediately flipping to the female figure. I stared at the naked woman, not caring about her arrows or the names of her parts, just that she was beautiful, and someday she would be me.

School Days

The blistering Phoenix summer days were a time of play, despite the yearly news story of a second string reporter literally frying an egg on the sidewalk. Children hurried outside minutes after finishing breakfast to meet their friends and wouldn't return until dinnertime, creating their fun, making up games. We ran through the streets at will, bounding over fences, cutting through yards, never caring or worrying about consequences. We were kids and these were our neighbors.

Sweltering afternoons were spent in the city pools followed by a bike ride through nearby Phoenix College, eluding campus security, who always managed to catch us at least once. We'd listen for the ice cream man at 3:25 p.m., the dime and nickel jangling in our pockets all day until we could spend it when the big white truck would pull up at its usual corner. Summer was a symbol of innocence, a season of youth and freedom, the time of growth and maturation that prepared us for the next school year.

No summer, though, could have prepared me for third grade and my math teacher, Mrs. Angle.

I hated everything about Mrs. Angle—the way she dressed, the way she talked, the fact that she looked just like George Washington on the dollar bill and most of all, I hated the endless word problems we did every day. Third grade had been easy until we started to do math without numbers. Most of our class, being *Sesame Street* protégés, had mastered the previous concepts taught by Mrs. Angle but this word problem stuff was a mystery.

"If Mrs. Smith buys two pounds of potatoes at thirty-nine cents a pound, and then buys one pound of apples at forty-nine cents a pound, how much will she have left from the five dollars she took with her to the market?" Mrs. Angle looked up from her book, her wrinkled face searching for an eager student to answer the question. Of course, no one volunteered. Big Bird never warned us about Mrs. Smith's produce predicaments.

While she waited for an answer that would never come willingly, she tapped her stubby fingers on the chalkboard and wiped her hands on the front of her black polyester dress, leaving lines of white chalk along her abdomen. Normally the class would have laughed at Mrs. Angle's "ghost streaks," but not today. We all knew whomever caught her eye would deal with Mrs. Smith. I felt my gaze pulled toward her dress. I had to see! So little in this class was enjoyable. I took what few pleasures I could get and seeing Mrs. Angle's chalk prints was very funny, especially since she was oblivious to the joke. The only thing funnier was when she leaned against the chalk tray and gave herself an equator ass. A chuckle forced its way through my throat and Mrs. Angle's radar honed in on me. "Kate Mitchell, why don't you give us the answer?"

My eyes darted back to the book and the stupid picture of Mrs. Smith standing at the fruit stand.

"Kate?"

It was too late. Simultaneously thirty pairs of eyes looked up. They were off the hook.

"Kate. I'm waiting." She walked to my desk, her middle jiggling under the polyester.

I shifted in my seat. The question was stupid. Why should I care about

Mrs. Smith's food purchases? I didn't even know what my own parents bought when we went shopping. I tried to focus on the problem. Forty-nine cents. Thirty-nine cents. Apples. Potatoes. Did it matter that it was potatoes? What if it had been tomatoes? Why do those words rhyme?

"Mrs. Angle, I have a question."

"What is that, dear?"

"Are you sure Mrs. Smith did her own shopping or did she have a maid?"

Mrs. Angle pursed her lips. "Kate, that question is inappropriate. You are being impertinent."

I was confused. "Is that good?"

Mrs. Angle's frown could have touched her shoes. "Young lady, you may go outside."

From that point on my problems with math and Mrs. Angle increased. During the next month I spent most of math class outside shooting craps with Mickey Cline. I didn't learn anything about word problems but I was getting really good at calculating probabilities. When Mrs. Angle finally realized I *liked* being sent outside, a parent-teacher-child conference was scheduled.

My parents were not thrilled, especially my mother. As a former teacher, she knew the drill. Parents are *never* called for a special conference to hear that their child is doing well. My mother spent the entire weekend before the Monday conference grilling me about my behavior, reminding me several times that I was a reflection on her. Translation: It doesn't look good when a former teacher, a molder and shaper of young minds, is raising a juvenile delinquent. Even on the way to the conference my mother was still snapping at me. I think my father was actually grateful because he was missing a boring meeting at work.

Once we got to Mrs. Angle's room, my mother attempted to speak their common teacher language but Mrs. Angle wasn't interested in building camaraderie with my mother.

"Now Mr. and Mrs. Mitchell, I don't mean to alarm you, but Kate has been having difficulty with word problems." Mrs. Angle adjusted her glasses and picked up my last test paper. "For example, when asked to calculate the speeds of two trains going from Los Angeles to New York, Kate responded, *'Take a plane'*."

My father stifled a laugh and Mom smacked him on the thigh.

Mrs. Angle's eyes wandered further down the test. "Here's an interesting one. Jogger A runs five miles per hour and Jogger B runs seven miles per hour. At these rates, how long will it take each of them to run thirty miles?"

My father leaned back in his chair. "That one's easy enough."

Mrs. Angle smiled victoriously. "I thought so myself. Kate, however, wrote, 'It depends on who brought a canteen. Even if Jogger B can run faster, if he didn't bring any water, he'll die.'" She let the test paper fall to the desk.

My mother sat stiffly in the small, wooden chair. She looked at me seriously. "Katie, dear, are these problems too hard?"

Why is it so important for adults to look good in front of each other in the presence of children? It was obvious each of them was contemplating cruel and horrible acts of child abuse to perform on my person. I knew what my mother was thinking. Teachers stick together. Yes, she was my mother, but at this moment, her sympathies lay with Mrs. Angle, educator of the ignorant, underpaid civil servant, and worst of all, an adult who had to put up with my crap.

"Katie, look at me." I gazed at my father, who smiled. "Tell me why you're writing these answers."

I shrugged my shoulders. I didn't know if I could do the problems. I wouldn't know how to begin to solve them.

My mother touched my arm. "Why don't we have Mrs. Angle help you with one right now?"

"Yes, Katie. Let's see you try," my father agreed.

"Very well," Mrs. Angle said. She motioned for me to sit next to her. She opened a math book and handed me a pencil. Please read number one out loud." I sighed deeply. I read fine. It was the math that was difficult. "Mrs. Jones takes ten dollars to the store. She spends one-half on meat, and one-fourth on vegetables. How much does she have left?"

"That's very good, Kate. Now, do you know what to do?"

I stared at the page. Visions of money, a huge ham shank, corn, peas and potatoes swirled in my brain. I saw the cute high school girl who worked in the produce department at FedMart deftly forming a tomato pyramid. I could never figure out how she got them to sit that way. And she was really cute.

Mrs. Angle coughed and a strong medicinal odor brought my mind back to the math cesspool I was currently swimming in. Damn my parents! Damn Mrs. Jones and her vegetables! Damn Mrs. Angle! I couldn't even remember the question.

"Now Kate, we went over this in class. Don't you remember?" Noticing my mental light bulb was not burning bright, my mother, ever the teacher, leaned closer. "Mrs. Angle, maybe if you wrote down the process, Kate could figure it out."

Mrs. Angle recoiled at the request. "The process?" she repeated.

"Of course. There's a process, a formula for everything in math," my mother stated, her level of frustration rising. So explain it." Her voice rose in pitch although she spoke barely above a whisper.

My father leaned forward in his chair as well, the wood creaking under his weight. Mrs. Angle's eyes shifted from my mother to father. She snatched the pencil from my hand. "Now Kate, follow closely. I'm only going through this one more time. Half of ten is five. Half of five is two-fifty. So five plus two-fifty equals seven-fifty, and seven-fifty from ten equals two-fifty." She quickly calculated the column and showed me the answer. Task accomplished. Another day's salary earned. I stared at the numbers, realizing this was all too complicated and I would never be able to function in a grocery store.

My father sat there rubbing his wide jaw. His gray eyes looked into mine. "Kate, do you understand?"

My gaze went from him to my mother to Mrs. Angle. Who could do me the most harm for the longest period of time? I nodded yes at my father, trying to salvage the rest of the year with Mrs. Angle.

His face hardened. "Honest?"

My eyes dropped to the floor. He had uttered the most sacred word in our house. Although I lied to my parents regularly about eating my vegetables and brushing my teeth, I never lied to them when they said the word *honest*. I shook my head no and thought of the seventy-three school days left. Seventy-three hours of torture I would now endure because I couldn't lie.

One question remained. What would my father do to me and Mrs. Angle? Math was extraordinarily important to an engineer. He had often told me that mathematical prowess (whatever that was) was crucial to success in college. Universities were impressed with good grades in algebra (some higher math thing) and high math scores on the SAT (a test that measured altitude).

There was no way Mrs. Angle and Mrs. Jones would separate me from college. The simplest thing in my mind would be to wipe her out. A huge man, my father could easily kill her with one swipe of his hand. I pictured her swinging from the intercom, the call button cord wrapped around her neck. Maybe he would just torture her until she promised to pass me despite my mathematical deficiencies. A few staples under the fingernails or sharpened pencils up the nose might make her more receptive to my plight.

I was very surprised to see my mother stand up first and put on her coat. Her movements were tight and quick. "Thank you for your time, Mrs. Angle. This has been a very enlightening discussion. Please know that I will be contacting the principal about this conference on Monday." Without shaking Mrs. Angle's hand, my mother turned on her heels and stormed out the door.

Mrs. Angle frowned at me. My poor parents, saddled with a mathematical idiot. My father tapped me on the shoulder. "Come on, Katie, let's not take up any more of Mrs. Angle's time."

I was a failure. My mother was furious with me and my father was disappointed in me. I couldn't do the math and they were humiliated. I was a stain on the family name, so much so that they were sending me to the principal, probably for a swat.

While we drove home my parents conversed quietly. We passed Phoenix College and I stared at the towering buildings, realizing I would probably never go to college because no school would ever accept me. Surely word problems were a requirement for admission.

Over the drone of the engine I heard very little of their conversation except words like *stupid* and *idiot* and I knew they were talking about me. As we pulled into the garage I clearly heard my mother say *old windbag* and I figured they'd changed topics, having said enough about my shortcomings as a math scholar. I waited all weekend for a punishment that never came.

On Monday my mother drove me to school and led me to Principal

Counts' office. I thought I would throw up. I waited in the chair outside, straining to listen to their conversation. My mother must have controlled her temper, because only once could I clearly hear when she said, "John, that woman is the worst math teacher I have ever seen. She's so far behind the times, and she's never bothered to catch up!"

At that moment Mrs. Angle appeared in front of me and knocked on the principal's door. She was scowling and I wasn't sure if it was because she had heard my mother or she just didn't like the sight of me.

The discussion remained cordial for almost an entire sixty seconds before Mrs. Angle's voice carried through the oak door.

"I have never been accused of such things in my entire career. Mrs. Mitchell, you are an overbearing parent who fails to recognize the inability of her little tomboy daughter. Perhaps if you spent more time making Kate into a lady and less time badgering teachers, Kate would be successful!"

"What does that have to do with anything?" my mother bellowed. "My daughter's physical appearance should have nothing to do with your ability *or lack thereof* to teach her mathematics."

"I don't have to listen to this!" Mrs. Angle exclaimed. The door flew open and her large rear end chugged past me. The principal appeared in the open doorway and smiled at me before he closed the door again. After Mrs. Angle's departure, there was no more screaming or yelling. I sat there and watched the clock.

"Hi," a voice said.

I looked over to the teacher mailboxes and saw a man retrieving his mail. He smiled at me and walked over to my chair. "Are you in trouble?" he asked dramatically.

I started to shake my head and then realized I had no idea if I was in any trouble, so I shrugged my shoulders. He started to laugh and it was contagious. We laughed together and I decided he had a nice laugh. He looked to be about my mom's age and he had bright blue eyes, and unlike most of the teachers who carried a briefcase, he had a backpack. He also didn't wear a tie like many of the other men, and instead of a suit, he had on a simple plaid shirt and khaki pants. He was different and I instantly liked him.

"What's your name?" He squatted down and met my gaze.

"I'm Kate," I answered, holding out my hand.

He nodded and met my handshake with a firm grasp. "I'm glad to make your acquaintance. I'm Mr. Andrews. Hey, Kate, do you like math?"

My face squinted into an unpleasant expression and he nodded. "I understand. It was hard for me too when I was your age."

Principal Counts opened his door. "Oh, Mr. Andrews, there you are. Will you come in please?"

Mr. Andrews stood up. "Hey, Kate, maybe I'll see you later. Would that be okay?"

I smiled and nodded my agreement.

Before he shut the door and entered the principal's office, he pointed at my feet. "I really like your cowboy boots."

That day marked the end of my career with Mrs. Angle. I transferred into Mr. Andrews's class and I soon learned that I was very far behind where I should have been. I began having tutoring sessions with my parents each night after the dinner dishes had been cleared. My father sat me down at the table and opened my math book. We worked for two solid hours on my homework and for some reason these problems weren't as difficult.

The after-dinner tutorials became a ritual, although at first I hated my father for making me miss all of the good TV shows. That changed as I watched my math grade skyrocket. By the end of the year, I had the third best math score in the class. My parents were thrilled, and my mother was ecstatic that my father had found something to do after dinner besides drink.

Mr. Andrews was one of those teachers who left an indelible impression on my memory and a firm imprint on my future career path. Of course, I remembered Mrs. Angle equally well. Just for all the wrong reasons.

September 10, 1972

Sister,

As promised, I have taken a few moments out of my busy work routine to pen another installment. Upon my untimely demise, (and any demise will be untimely), I want you to arrange my letters and publish them under the title, The Life and Times of Charles Driscoll OR How to Turn Degenerate Irresponsibility into an Art Form. *I think it would be appropriate to have a commentary written by a psychoanalyst or a defrocked priest.*

I have managed to take a job as a projectionist at a place called Portofinos, which specializes in films of a rather erotic nature. Suffice to say, you can never bring your children to see Uncle at work. Don't bother to tell Mom, since I'm sure she won't approve and I've given up trying to explain why I'm not you.

I know I could pick up the phone and call but I prefer to write. My preference is based, in part, on the fact that I spend seven hours per day, six days per week in this damn theatre, and as a consequence I have a lot of time on my hands. *Much of my time is spent reading and writing (I am presently creating an involved theory that mankind is inferior to the Venus flytrap). At other times I make obscene phone calls to Nestor but he's starting to like them.*

I don't know how much you know about my abrupt departure from the Old Pueblo of Tucson, but I left one afternoon to get a pack of cigarettes and never returned. Now such behavior may subject me to ugly epithets, but if the incident is seen in relation to the rest of my behavior, it is not only predictable, but commendable—in so far as consistency is a virtue. My wife, who undoubtedly will soon be my ex-wife, is better off without me, as are my children.

The next day I hitched a ride into Tempe. I couldn't find a place to stay, so I slept under various bushes near Arizona State. (I recommend the evergreens near the Newman Center).

One day I ran into Trevor Zambrowski III. At one point he ran a newspaper in California, but after falling victim to the drink, he now runs a paper route for the Tempe Daily News. *Through him I met Gerry Marks. Gerry was tending bar in Tempe and I asked her if she wouldn't mind if I camped out in her backyard. The ASU police were becoming suspicious of the snoring hedge at the Newman Center. Gerry said not only could I stay but she'd do me one better—I could stay in the large school bus in her backyard.*

Gerry is an attractive forty-year-old with four children (ages nine to seventeen) who is majoring in nutrition at ASU. Also living with her is Tom, an eighteen-year-old cripple, a beautiful sixteen-year-old runaway named Natalie and an outrageously alcoholic school teacher named Joy. Gerry's oldest son, Greg, had gotten into drugs and when she learned that I had worked as a drug counselor, she invited me to stay with her menagerie. She said she wanted a man around the house. Blushing appropriately, I told her I would be glad to come.

I must say I've enjoyed filling you in on my recent activities. Emerson teaches that when you write for your own pleasure, you are assured an eternal audience. Give my love to Joe and I hope he doesn't have trouble with his engineering licensing exams. I, myself, have had little trouble over the years gaining whatever license I have wanted, poetic or otherwise.

Keeping all my fingers and toes crossed,
Charlie

The Omniscient Omnipotent

Third grade will always be remembered as the most trying of my educational years, mainly because of Mrs. Angle but also because of Sister Mary Elizabeth Donahue, my C.C.D. teacher. Besides enduring Mrs. Angle five days a week, I got the privilege of sitting through ninety minutes of instruction from the oldest nun on the face of the earth, a nun who believed Vatican II and the twentieth century had never occurred.

Catholic Christian Doctrine is a fancy name for Sunday school. Every week after Mass, I and the other eight-year-old martyrs suffered under Sister Mary's tutelage, learning what we'd done to deserve the fiery pits of hell or what we'd do to get there. She tried her best to scare us but no one took her seriously. What could happen if we misbehaved or didn't do our homework? She could throw us out but most of us were already saying novenas, hoping that would happen.

The only real leverage she had against us was our parents, but since most of them had experienced C.C.D., they were tacitly sympathetic, insisting that we go but understanding that it was to follow church doctrine and ease their soaring Catholic guilt. Thus, by divine perpetual motion, I found myself facing Sister Mary every Sunday, a rather unpleasant sight on the Lord's Day.

We called her Scary Mary. Her face reminded me of a Rand/McNally road map, a bunch of bisecting lines with a few points of interest along the way, most especially her eyes. They receded back into her head, making the sockets appear large and empty. As for the rest of her body, who knew? She could have been a Minotaur underneath her robe and no one would have suspected.

As third graders, it was Scary's responsibility to prepare us for the third of the Seven Sacraments—confession—which required eight-year-olds to sit in a tiny, dark room whose only furniture was a kneeler facing a small, curtained window. The priest sat in an adjacent room and when he heard a confessor enter, he slid the partition open but kept the curtain drawn. The confession could be heard, but the identity of the sinner remained anonymous. I still remember the claustrophobic feeling that came over me every time I knelt in the confessional. Only in the name of God could a child be locked in a closet for his own good.

As Sister Mary explained the concept of listing our sins for Father Horton and his assignment of penance, the class was enthralled. Sister Mary assured us that Father Horton received divine guidance and that our punishments for offending the Lord were sound.

Pretty Alicia Walker looked up, her eyes popping out of her head. "You mean God talks to Father Horton?"

"Of course," Sister Mary twittered. Although she looked like a hag, Sister Mary had the voice of a bird.

"Why doesn't he talk to me?" Joey Doogle stammered.

"Because you are not a priest."

"Does he talk to you, Sister Mary?" Alicia asked.

Sister Mary stuck her hands in her robe and paced the floor. "Well Alicia, God talks to me but it's not the same. Priests have a direct link to the Almighty, something the rest of us lack."

Joey Doogle almost leapt out of his chair. "You mean like a hotline to God? Like the red phone the president carries around?"

"Exactly," Sister Mary exclaimed. She had to be thrilled. This was the most excited anyone in the class had ever been about anything.

"So if I became a priest, I could talk to God too!" Joey shouted.

"Of course," Sister Mary agreed, already picturing Joey in his vestments.

Joey slugged me in the arm. "Ha, ha, Katie! I can be a priest and you can't. Ha!"

I shot out of my chair, ready to pummel him. "You shut up, Joey. I can do anything you can do!" I turned toward Sister Mary for affirmation. "I could be a priest, couldn't I, Sister Mary?"

She sighed. "No, Katie. The priesthood is for men only. Women become nuns." A touch of remorse permeated her voice.

I stamped my foot. "But I want to be a priest!"

"Now Katie, you can be a nun," she said patiently.

"But I can't be a priest." I slumped back into my chair and forgot where I was. "That's a pisser."

Sister Mary's face turned dark brown. Some people turn red when they're furious but Scary looked like she'd just come back from vacation in Florida. A long finger emerged from the robe and pointed at me.

"Kate Mitchell, you will not say that word again in this class. And I expect you to tell Father Horton about your foul mouth next week during confession."

I assumed a penitent pose, bowing my head and staring at my desk all the while thinking about what a stupid religion I was stuck in. I could be a much better priest than Joey—he was so damn klutzy. He'd probably drop the baby the first time he performed a baptism. It seemed so unfair and I knew it was wrong. I'd heard a woman named Gloria Steinem talk about something called *sexism*. I wasn't sure I totally understood it but I was pretty sure she wasn't Catholic.

There was something else that really bothered me. Sister Mary had said that God talked to Father Horton. It didn't take a genius to understand the implications. God knew everything, which meant that if God was a blabbermouth, then Father Horton knew everything too. This scared the hell out of me. I thought of the multitude of sins I'd committed just in the past week. I thought of the donuts Robby Wentworth and I had stolen last week during fellowship session. Then there was Janie Freeman's Barbie doll, now burned beyond recognition and hiding under my bed. What about the pet lizard I'd secretly been keeping in my dresser drawer? It was amazing Father Horton had time to say Mass in the midst of tallying my transgressions alone.

And what about past sins? I thought of Robby and me in the bathroom.

And Kimmie Lancaster.

Sister Mary had once mentioned "homo somethings" and said they were the worst type of sinners. At the time I'd thought of Kimmie Lancaster but I couldn't remember why.

My hand shot up in the air. "Sister Mary?"

Sister Mary ignored my violent waving until she'd finished telling a story about a little boy who'd gone to hell. "Yes, Katie?"

My heart thumped. "Sister Mary, you said God talked to Father Horton, right?"

Her face browned. "Yes, Katie, that is correct."

"And God knows everything?"

She noticed my panicked expression and at first looked puzzled but then a slight smile crossed her face as our minds met. "Yes, Katie, *everything.*"

By Sunday I was an emotional disaster. I had spent the entire week thinking of confession and terrorizing my family and friends, hoping to camouflage my thoughts of Kimmie Lancaster with these recent sins. I prayed I was right, otherwise the three weeks grounding I'd received for jumping off the roof and into the mulberry tree would be in vain.

As I waited my turn to enter the confessional, I wrung my hands and stared at the enormous crucifix above the altar. The other kids ahead of me had made lists of their sins, unaware that Father Horton already knew what they would say. I watched them read and reread their papers, attempting to commit the sins to memory before they entered the dark closet.

Joey Doogle exited the confessional, mumbling his penance over and over. Penance was the other thing that worried me. What would be my punishment? Would this involve physical labor? Would it affect my allowance? What if I couldn't do the penance? Would I have to go back to confession?

Before I realized what was happening, I'd entered the confessional.

While the door was open, the room didn't seem so bad but as I knelt, the door swung shut and the room turned black. I could hear myself breathing and the faint murmur of Father Horton talking to the sinner on the other side. My eyes adjusted and I looked around the confessional, straining to see what lurked in the corners. I thought of two glimmering eyes, God's eyes. Grandma always said God made his presence known when you least expected him to. I wondered if that was how he knew everything, by hiding in the shadows and lurking in closets.

It occurred to me that God must be pretty busy. There was a good chance that he could only talk to Father Horton once in a while. Since there were lots of other priests, surely Father Horton wasn't the only one talking to God. I sighed with relief as I pictured God with his Priest Yellow Pages in hand and the phone cradled against his ear.

I was so deep in thought that I didn't hear the window slide open. The patient Father must have sat there for a good minute before saying, "Hello? Is anyone there?"

I nearly fell off the kneeler at the sound of his baritone voice. It made me wonder if I wasn't speaking to the Almighty himself. This was a possibility I hadn't explored. Maybe God possessed Father Horton during confession, just like in that book *The Exorcist* (a book I wasn't even supposed to touch but had during my rampant sin spree that week).

He waited. I waited. He coughed. "You may begin, my child."

My mind went blank. This was like some horrible test. "Uh-uh," I stammered.

He took pity on me and gave me the first line. "Bless me father, for I have sinned."

I continued and things were going smoothly until we got to the actual confessing part. I didn't know what to say but I certainly knew what I wasn't going to say. "Uh, Father, if you're a priest, don't you already know my sins?"

He coughed. "What do you mean, my child?"

"Well, Sister Mary said you talked with God and since he knows all our sins, I thought he would have told you before I got here."

More coughing. "Well, what Sister Mary meant was . . ." He sighed. "Why don't you refresh my memory?"

"Oh, okay." I hadn't counted on Father Horton being forgetful. "I said pisser to Sister Mary. She told me to tell you that."

"And a good thing you did."

I rattled off the many childhood pranks I'd pulled that week and I wondered if I should mention the donut heist.

"Is that all my child?"

"Father, can I confess someone else's sins?"

"What?" he exclaimed.

"Robby Wentworth stole four donuts during fellowship last week."

"Oh, he did, did he?"

"Yeah, two Boston cream, a glazed and a chocolate honey dipped. I was, I mean, he was going to take more but Mr. Mathers turned around."

"Why did Robby take *four* donuts?"

"He was hungry?"

"I don't think so," Father Horton replied. "I think you stole those donuts and you feel guilty."

I pictured his steel eyes staring at me, just like they had last year when a few of us put milk in the holy water.

"Katie, are you all right?"

"Yes, father." I opened my mouth, but nothing else came out. He'd said my name!

"Katie, you stole those donuts, didn't you?"

"Yes, father," I whispered.

"Very well. Say three Hail Marys and two Our Fathers."

"Yes, father."

"And in the future, Katie, do not steal and do not lie."

I nodded, forgetting he couldn't see me. He started to shut the window.

"Father!"

The window stopped. I could see his silhouette clearly. "Yes, my child?"

"How did you know it was me?"

There was a long pause. "How do you think I knew?"

I gasped, ran out of the confessional and slammed the door. Several of the other children stared at me and the next student opened the door carefully, wondering what lurked on the other side.

I leaned against the wall for a few seconds. When I finally started breathing again, I heard laughter. Someone must have been confessing something really funny, because Father Horton was laughing hysterically.

March 7, 1974

Sis,

Not a lot has happened, but I managed to get to a party for my friend, Beulah, at the 6 West Motel. Decorations were up and Beulah's sister, Zelda, had prepared a giant sheet cake. A grand sentimental touch had been added: in the middle of the cake, wrapped in tin foil, was Morris's .44 Magnum revolver. Morris was Beulah's old love and it used to tickle her pink the way Morris would shoot up their old haunt, Jerry's Bar. Beulah cried and cried at the sight of a hundred beastly drunks, dopers, bikers, prostitutes, freaks, hard hats and numerous other persona non grata, breaking into song.

The only mar on the evening occurred when two well dressed gentlemen approached me, identified themselves as FBI agents and asked me outside. Bubba, a former member of the Insane Leather Bikers, grabbed me and shouted that they would never take me alive. I disengaged myself from Bubba and went to the parking lot, where the agents asked me if I knew a guy named CJ. It seemed a few weeks before, the windows of the Tempe City

Hall had been shot out and they had traced the trajectory of the bullets to the house I rent from my friend Gerry. Apparently Gerry's arch-criminal son was out of town, so that left me and CJ, who'd been staying with Gerry. CJ is a seventeen-year-old runaway who joined Gerry's zoo. A good kid, except that he's a master thief and he's got a thing for city halls.

While I was talking with the agents, Bubba gathered a group of his brothers together and they offered to shoot the agents but I diplomatically declined. I also rejected their offer to shoot me, lest I suffer the indignation of arrest. Since I could prove my whereabouts, the agents prepared to leave. I don't blame them for being anxious. The crowd in the parking lot had become a mob of surly drunks. Even Beulah started taking the tin foil off the revolver. Everyone screamed when the agents drove off and we went inside to celebrate the birth of my new dossier in Washington, DC.

Oh what a life. Why don't you ask Father Smith if there's a parish that needs a gardener? I think I could handle it—except for spring.

Enough for now. I often wonder if I can get pregnant from sleeping at Portofinos.

See you at the movies!
Charlie

Bingo

"Do you see any, Katie?"

"Not yet." A small white sphere rolled toward the flagged hole. "There's one."

"How far?"

"About ten feet."

"Hmm . . . that's a good shot. What do you want to do?"

"Ah, let's give it to him."

Grandma laughed. "Okay."

I rushed onto the green, dropped the golf ball into the hole and rushed back to our cart, which we'd hidden in a grove of trees. Somebody would be really surprised.

We waited for the unsuspecting golfer. As we watched through the tangle of bushes, a rear end covered in lime green golf pants hovered over the hole. When he saw his unbelievable shot, he started to laugh, a huge hyena laugh.

Grandma scowled. "Oh, hell." She threw the cart into gear and we sputtered along the fairway.

"What's wrong, Grandma?"

"I'd know that laugh anywhere. That's Melvin Gould. He's the last person I'd like to see get a hole-in-one."

"Why Grandma?"

"He's a prick."

"What's a prick?"

She did a double take. "Never mind. And don't tell your mother I said that."

I loved spending the weekend with Grandma. She let me do anything I wanted and she was eager to corrupt me and lead me down the path of sin. Her five-foot, ninety-pound frame was deceptive. People took one look at this slight, pretty lady and attached words like demure and flowery to her character. That quickly changed after a string of obscenities escaped her mouth. My grandmother loved to swear and my mother blamed her for my propensity to do the same.

Mary Margaret Lacey had been a flapper in the speakeasies during the Twenties, worked with the early feminist movement and chased fire engines as a way to meet men. Ironically she wound up marrying a police officer. On her way to a fire one day, Grandpa pulled Grandma over for speeding. She tried to talk her way out of it but she got the ticket and six months later she got a proposal.

Despite her wild ways, Grandma settled down with Grandpa, raised two children and saw Grandpa through a terrible, debilitating bout of arthritis that killed him before I was born. I'm sure she missed Grandpa but Grandma was a free spirit and comfortable with just about anybody.

Spending the weekend with her was always a treat and the highlight of our weekends together was always bingo. Being old and Catholic, it was expected that Grandma would attend Saturday night bingo at her church. Grandma always sat next to her best friend, Tatyana Wojtulewicz, a powder keg in a wheelchair. Her friends called her T, and she really was hell on wheels. She was the biggest gossip in all of Sun City, their adult community. It was rumored she had dirt on everyone, including Father Fields. T grew up in Poland during World War II. She had hundreds of stories about Poland before Hitler's invasion. She could knit a great yarn but they all ended with her face turning red before she blurted, "And then those damn Nazis took over!" T hated the Nazis.

She reminded me of a hot fudge sundae. Her body was like scoops of ice cream piled on top of each other. A brown wig perched on her head, complete with a red bow. Grandma and T were both sixty-five, but neither looked it. Grandma still got carded when she tried to get a senior citizen's discount and T was a walking corpse.

Since Grandma insisted on sitting next to T, I was forced to endure the company of Grandma's other closest friend, Adelaide Portnoy. Adelaide used to work for Mary Kay cosmetics and apparently she had never turned in her makeup case. She wore more face goo than anyone I'd ever seen and by the end of the evening, I was usually wearing a good deal of it too. The only thing that made Adelaide bearable was the dollar she gave me before we went home.

Across the table sat the Finns and Mr. Rock. The Finn sisters were old maids who'd made a fortune in the stock market before insider trading was illegal. They looked almost exactly alike, except Maude Finn was five years older than Esther Finn, a fact that Maude constantly harped on, drawing Esther's ire. Bernard Rock reminded me of Mr. Clean, with his solid features and muscular body. He looked like a geriatric GQ model and he abhorred polyester and loud prints. I liked him and I knew Grandma did too. She was always winking at him and patting him on the arm.

After my customary kiss from Adelaide, the bingo began. The Finns were in full form, having ignited their argument in the car on the way over. Grandma and Mr. Rock exchanged smiles and we all prepared our cards.

Father Fields adjusted his microphone and waited for the reverb to stop. "Our first number is B-seven. B-seven."

I had B-seven on all three cards.

"Maude, you've already made a mistake," Esther chided. "You missed B-seven on your center card." Esther reached for Maude's card and Maude slapped her hand.

"Esther Finn, you keep your hands off of my cards. That's illegal."

"What are you talking about, Maude?"

"I-eighteen. I-eighteen."

"Everybody knows that tampering with bingo cards is a punishable offense."

"That's the mail, stupid."

"Margaret, you tell Esther. Tell her about bingo law."

My grandmother ignored them. We all enjoyed listening to the sisters but nobody wanted to come between them.

"B-nine. B-nine."

"What is it with all these B's?" T declared.

"O-seventy-two. O-seventy-two."

"Now, seventy-two. That was a good year," Esther announced.

Maude raised an eyebrow. "Do you mean eighteen seventy-two, or nineteen seventy-two, sister, dear?"

"You were the only one alive who'd know the difference, Maude," Esther spat.

"N-thirty-two. N-thirty-two."

"Now, Esther Finn, I've had enough of your lip tonight."

Mr. Rock groaned. "Ladies, please. I can't hear the numbers."

"Well, if you'd quit looking at Margaret, you'd probably concentrate better," T retorted.

Mr. Rock and Grandma stared at T "T, is something bothering you, dear?" Grandma's voice dripped with goodwill.

"G-fifty-eight. G-fifty-eight."

T scanned her cards, pretending not to hear Grandma. I'd pretty much forgotten the game, seeing how the conversation was so lively.

"T, I asked you a question," Grandma pressed.

"We all know about you and Bernard, Margaret. Why do you bother trying to hide it?"

"Hide what?" Grandma asked innocently. Mr. Rock was pale.

"The fact that he's dipping his wick into you every Wednesday afternoon."

"What?" Adelaide gasped.

"T, that's none of your business!" Mr. Rock exclaimed.

"I-twenty. I-twenty."

My grandmother pointed a wary finger at T "I advise you to keep your nose out of my affairs, Tatyana Wojtulewicz, or you may find it broken."

T glared at Grandma. "Is that a threat, Margaret?"

"No, that's a promise. Don't you remember last year? You opened your big mouth about my new dentures and you paid. Do you remember that?"

"How could I forget? You painted my dear Princess silver! It took weeks for that paint to wear off." Princess was T's cat.

"N-forty. N-forty."

"So you know to mind your own beeswax. What goes on between Bernard and me is our business." I noticed Mr. Rock got paler every time his name was mentioned.

"What about between Bernard and Sylvia Ormsby? Do you care about that?" T grinned, rather pleased with herself as she blacked out her N-forties.

Mr. Rock stiffened. "T, nothing happened between me and Sylvia, and you know that."

"That's not what I heard," T retorted. "I heard you dropped Bible study on Thursday evenings for her."

"Mrs. Ormsby needed someone to drive her to rehabilitation on Thursday nights. I thought the good Lord wouldn't mind."

"I-twenty-three. I-twenty-three."

"Oh, I know all that," T continued. "But Mary Lou Jessup says you'd go into Sylvia's place after you all got back and you'd be there for some time."

"She offered me coffee!"

"N-35. N-35."

T shook her head. By now, the only ones really playing bingo were the Finns and Adelaide. Grandma turned to T and stood up.

"Tatyana Wojtulewicz, I'm only going to say this once. I know all about Bernard and Sylvia Ormsby. And if Mary Lou Jessup had better eyesight, she'd know that on a few of those Thursday nights I went with them to the rehab center! Now if you don't close your mouth right now, I'm going to do it for you!" Grandma had leaned into T, gripping the arms of the wheelchair.

"How dare you use that tone with me, Margaret Lacey!" T shifted into gear and drove over Grandma's foot. I watched the pain register on Grandma's face as T tore off down the aisle.

"I-twenty-five. I-twenty-five."

"Bingo!" Adelaide cried. She threw her arms around me and planted a big kiss on my cheek. I could feel the oily lipstick on my skin. It was gross.

The cheers of the crowd drowned out Grandma's scream—and her cussing. But once everyone stopped applauding and Adelaide made her way to the front for her twenty-five-dollar prize, Grandma's voice was clearly audible.

"Goddamn you, T Wojtulewicz! I'm going to whip your sorry ass into tomorrow if it's the last thing I do!" Grandma weaved through the rows of people, chasing T's wheelchair. Although T had a head start, Grandma was quick. All that tennis and golf paid off. She had T cornered by the refreshment table.

"You think you're so much better than the rest of us, Miss High and Mighty? Just because you happen to be chairman of the All Saints Committee? Well, let me tell you something, missy, there's more to life than God!" She quickly turned to the podium. "Sorry, Father." Father Fields nodded weakly.

"And if Bernard Rock wants to dip his wick every day of the year, it's fine with me!"

I looked at Mr. Rock. He was green.

"But then you wouldn't know a damn thing about that, now would you? The last time you had any goodies was VJ Day! And no wonder! You wear this goddamn rug on your head. You think it makes you look young? It makes you look like some old fart with a wig on her head!"

Grandma grabbed T's wig and held it up in the air. The crowd gasped and T started to cry. She buried her nearly bald scalp in her hands. Grandma sighed, plopped the wig back on top of T's head and came back to our table.

T maneuvered her squeaky wheels back to her spot. She tried to straighten the clump of hair but it was pointless. T didn't look at Grandma and Grandma didn't look at her. I knew this wouldn't last long. By tomorrow they'd be on the phone apologizing, if they didn't do it tonight.

Finally, Father Fields broke the silence and called for a nice game of four corners. We all got into it again and I prayed Adelaide didn't win anymore that night. I had one clean cheek and wanted to keep it that way.

By nine o'clock everything was forgotten and we all had a good time—except for Mr. Rock. He just sat there staring at his cards.

"Grandma," I said, whispering into her ear. "Is Mr. Rock all right?"

Grandma glanced up and looked at Mr. Rock's well-defined body, a smile creeping over her face. "Don't worry about him, honey. It's nothing a Wednesday afternoon can't fix."

January 19, 1975

Dear Sis,

Since I have another slow day on my hands here at the theatre (known in the trade as a PORN-MORN), I thought I'd relate to you the events over Christmas Eve.

I had worked at the theatre all day, and as usual found my way to Jerry's Bar. The bartender, Big John, filled my glass with 151 proof rum and it was not long before Bing Crosby's "White Christmas" had assumed new dimensions of meaning for me. I was well on my way to obliteration, when Gary, Gerry's son, said she needed me at the house.

When I arrived, my highly sophisticated powers of observation took immediate notice of the eight supine figures so tastefully draped and otherwise scattered about the living room. They wore sleeveless jean jackets of a local motorcycle club, the name of which I discreetly preserve in my memory alone.

It occurred to me that these gentlemen had been overwhelmed by the sentiment of the holiday. Gerry was in the kitchen, and upon seeing me, ran into another room (I affect a lot of women this way). She reappeared, and pressing a small fruitcake and a revolver into my hand, said, "GET THEM OUT OF HERE!"

I had neither the why or wherefore to question her motives, so, with some difficulty, I managed to get the indelicate eight out onto the front lawn. It was at that time I discovered how manipulative people are on Christmas Eve. In spite of their poetic rejoinders (Fuck YOU, Shove It), I insisted that they arrange themselves in a proper order, whereupon we marched over to the Tempe Police Department.

Now I really love to sing Christmas carols and because I love it so much, others around me love it too—or so I am convinced when I drink 151 proof rum.

Anyway, we sang "God Rest Ye Merry Gentlemen," "Noel," "Joy to the World" and finished with "Silent Night."

All of the bikers were in excellent voice and most of them remembered most of the lyrics. Only one of us was arrested. Straight Stan Manny insisted on giving the desk sergeant a hit of Christmas Nembutal. It was a fine Christmas Eve.

Barbara, I feel compelled to respond to your Christmas gift. I know what you mean when you speak of our "strong bond of friendship." I can even remember when I started liking you. Your kind words have shown me to feel just how real that bond is. I think that element was missing in my marriage— friendship. Essential to friendship is faith and my lifestyle, my habits, do very little to encourage anyone in my immediate company to have much faith in me. The problem is compounded by the fact that I am inclined to accept most people on their terms and I find that such acceptance is frequently translated as indifference. Ergo, I am self-centered, cold, indifferent and utterly lacking in the most noble of all human virtues—guilt.

Whatever the case, I give you thanks for the finest Christmas present I, or any creature, have ever received.

Merry Christmas and Happy New Year,
Charles

Present Day

We've barely walked through the front door after attending Cousin Margaret's funeral when the phone rings. I slip off my shoes while my partner Sarah answers the call. Seven-year-old Luke beelines for his room and the TV, eager to shed his dress clothes and forget about dead people.

"Uh-huh, I see. I'll tell her." She clicks the handset off and looks empathetically at me. "The nurse says you need to go to the care center. Your mother is refusing to get out of the car and they can't force her because that would be abusive."

I sigh and encase my feet in the dress shoes once again. "Do you want me to come with you?" she asks.

I shake my head and grab my purse. "I'm sure she's just upset about Margaret's funeral. I can't imagine what it must have been like for her or what she was thinking."

"Call me if you need me," Sarah says, kissing me on the lips.

When I arrive in the parking lot, a small crowd has gathered around my father's Buick. Three of the workers dressed in brightly colored scrubs hover over an empty wheelchair, the supposed occupant still stubbornly sitting in the Buick, which is quickly turning into an oven. My father leans inside the open passenger door, attempting to coax my mother out, while my brother sits in the driver's seat, keeping the car running and the air conditioning going.

"Maybe you can talk to her," my father says, sweat pouring from his face. It is noontime in the middle of July and with the exception of the care center workers, we are all dressed in our Sunday best to honor our late cousin. His temper rests in his jawline and his face twitches as he controls his anger.

I bend down, a burst of air conditioning slapping me in the face. Heat has always been my mother's enemy and she is starting to wheeze, the portable oxygen tank running low. She wears a simple dress covered in flowers but her hair is pasted to her scalp and droplets of perspiration settle into the lines of her face. The red lipstick, the only makeup she wears, slices across her face, an aberration against her pale skin.

"Hi, Mom. Why are you still outside? Why don't we go inside?"

"No, I'm not going in."

"Mom, it's really hot out here. We need to get you indoors and get you a cool drink. Don't you want a drink?"

"No, I'm fine."

"Mom, you can't stay out here. It's too hot. You'll make yourself sick."

My mother looks at me as though I'm an idiot and unable to understand English. "I'm not going inside. I'm waiting to go."

I know that when she says *go*, she means go home. I avoid that conversation and take a different approach. "No, we already went Mom. We went to the funeral and now we're back."

"Where?"

"To where you live."

"I'm not here. I'm not staying."

"Why not?"

"I'm not. I don't belong there."

I take a breath, my father's temperament contagious and genetically inherited. This conversation is going nowhere and we're all being victimized by the summer sun. My mother, as illogical as she is speaking, actually makes total sense. "Mom, I'd really like to get you a cool drink. Let's go. They're right over there."

"I'll bet you would."

She has seen through my trickery. I laugh at how sharp her mind can be at times. At this point I start pulling my mother's legs from the car because even if the attendants can't force my mother from the car, I can.

"No, don't do that. Stop! I'm not going back there!" she cries.

"Mom, I can't have you get sick," I say in my most pleasant voice. My father takes her arms, and while she fights back in her mind, physically, she is no match. The Herculean-size guilt my father carries wouldn't allow him to physically remove her from the car but now that someone else is willing to wear the black hat, he readily helps.

"No! Don't do this to me! I don't belong here! You can't make me go! Stop!"

Once we have her halfway out of the car, the attendants take over, also using their most soothing, caring words. They move her to the wheelchair despite her vehement protests.

"I'm not going to forget this! No, siree. I'm not," she says, glaring at me and my father. I notice my brother continues to hide in the car, escaping her wrath. They wheel her inside and I turn to my father and give him a hug. He's aged tremendously since losing my mother's everyday companionship. They held each other up for forty years and the stress of facing life without her has consumed him.

He shakes his head, all of our frustration melting in the heat. "I think the funeral really got to her."

I nod, feeling a lump forming in my throat. "I'll call you later," I say, hugging him again. I wave at my brother and head back out to the street and my car, my mother's words and her tone of betrayal replaying in my mind.

Conscientious Objector

People remember two things about Athena Witherspoon—she was athletic and she was black. No one remembers her grades or her offensive personality, only those two facts. She came to Wright Elementary in the middle of fourth grade and instantly assumed the position of best female athlete, a title I usually shared with my best friend A.J.

What began as envy quickly turned to dislike. Athena loved to put others down. She gave people nicknames like Larry the Lisp and Fatboy. Her favorite target was Angus Young, the class geek who loved to study insects. She tortured Angus about his strange hobby but mostly about his wardrobe.

Angus's clothes were Salvation Army rejects. His parents never graduated from high school and they worked in a fast-food restaurant for a paycheck only slightly above minimum wage. On their menial salaries, they raised three boys, Angus being the youngest. All of his clothes were hand-me-downs and they rarely fit him since his brothers were built like high-rise towers and Angus was more like a mini-mall. His brothers, Enoch and Farley, were twice as big as Angus and athletically gifted. Enoch was football and Farley was basketball. Angus was the runt, the recessive gene. He got the brains while his brothers got the brawn and because of this unfair distribution of power, he swallowed Athena's abuse daily.

On this, the first day of fifth grade, Angus actually looked presentable but Athena noticed his pants were too short and rode above his ankles. She pointedly asked, "Where's the flood, Arachnoid?"

Angus uncrossed his legs, hoping his pants would lengthen and cover his stark white tube socks. Before another comment could pass through her lips, A.J. zapped her with a spitball and Athena slumped in her chair. She glared at us and we glared at her. It was going to be a long year.

In retrospect, Athena was a mystery and a novelty. Most of us suburban kids had never really known a black person. For me and Angus, though, the novelty wore off around Thanksgiving.

A.J. agreed to help us carry out our revenge.

For a week the three of us met every day after school at Angus's favorite bug spot. My queasiness about insects quickly evaporated and my enthusiasm grew with each bug I collected. By Friday our backs and necks ached from spending the entire week stooped over in a ball, staring at the ground and plucking bugs from their habitat. It was worth it when Angus called me Sunday night and stated that he had chloroformed six hundred ants, moths, crickets, roaches, beetles and several other types of creepy crawlies I couldn't name.

We met Monday morning by the olive tree. Angus opened the plastic trash bag and showed us the multitude of remains. I thought I was going to be sick. Alive the creatures hadn't been so bad but dead was a different story. We hid the bag in the tree until later that day. Every time I looked at Athena, I smiled. I started to feel a little guilty around noon, but then she called Carol Johnson a bastard and anger overtook guilt. Athena was going to get it good.

During afternoon recess, Angus got the bag while A.J. and I acted as lookouts. Mr. Duncan always left the room open while he went to the lounge for a smoke. We snuck back in and filled Athena's desk with the corpses, placing Angus's pet mouse Einstein (who just happened to conveniently expire the previous weekend) on top of the heap. It was disgusting. Most everything Athena owned was covered by beady little eyes, antennae, fuzzy legs and hard shells. Only the edge of her protractor protruded from the upper corner of her desk.

After recess Mr. Duncan asked us to take out our spelling books. Athena was so busy chastising Herman West for his poor kickball abilities that she didn't even notice the bugs as she stuck her hand deep into the desk. This was an added bonus. We'd never thought Athena would actually touch the bugs. We watched her swirl the carcasses around, too busy talking to notice what she was doing. Grabbing the spelling book, she turned to see her hand buried in the disgusting bug stew. The scream was deafening. She jumped out of her chair, flinging bugs everywhere. Several curious students rushed to Athena's desk, and upon seeing the sight, let out screams of their own. Many ran from the room and one girl fainted.

Angus, A.J. and I just sat there laughing. Mr. Duncan came over and surveyed the situation. Even a greenhorn like Mr. Duncan could figure this one out. He sent a hysterical Athena to the nurse, calmed the other students and took the three of us outside while the rest of the class watched through the windows.

"Judging from your reactions, can I assume you are responsible for this?" Mr. Duncan was a young, progressive teacher who didn't believe in talking down to children. We didn't say anything and kept our eyes focused on the grass. "Do you realize what you've done? You've traumatized this poor girl—"

"But she's horrible!"

I looked around because I didn't recognize the voice. Seeing only the four of us, my gaze settled on Angus, his body shaking and his fists clenched. His stance suggested he might hit Mr. Duncan at any time but his eyes, clouded with tears, showed his true pain and unhappiness. He wanted to cry but his hatred prevented him from doing so.

Mr. Duncan tried to hug Angus but Angus stepped back stiffly, his eyes focused on something in his brain. Instinct told Mr. Duncan to leave Angus alone. He stood immobile until his parents came, escorted by the principal and the school nurse. It was only after several minutes of gentle words from his mother that Angus unclenched his fists. His parents led him through the breezeway to their car, each with a hand on his shoulder. That was the last time I ever saw Angus. There were rumors that he'd gone crazy but actually he'd just transferred to another school in the district. For him, there were no punishments, no repercussions.

A.J. and I were different. Criticism and jokes rolled off our backs, and our biting retorts kept everyone, even Athena, from picking on us too much. The administration wondered why we'd involved ourselves in such a devious act. There could only be one answer—we were prejudiced. No one ever thought we just might be helping Angus since he never would have done anything alone. No one remembered that I had defended Angus against other students previously. No, we must be prejudiced and this was a kiddie version of a KKK lynching. So besides serving a month of detention, A.J. and I had to write letters of apology to the Witherspoon family and worst of all, we had to meet with the school counselor, Mrs. Neal.

Known as the "head shrinker" by most of the student body, Marjorie Neal was the district's roving psychologist, visiting several different grade schools during the week. I'd only met her once, during second grade when a classmate died in a car accident. She came in during math class, asked, "Is everyone doing all right?" and left when no one looked up.

I didn't have a lot of faith in Mrs. Neal's counseling abilities. Normally she only saw two Wright Elementary students consistently, Wayne Toliver and Linda Stevens. Wayne spent most of his academic life making paper clip sculptures of his teachers and Linda was "emotionally disturbed." After a year of counseling, I didn't see any change in Wayne's behavior, except that his sculptures were getting really lifelike. And as for Linda, I would have bet money that she'd have been less "disturbed" if her daddy stopped molesting her every Saturday night.

So early Monday morning, the school secretary led me into Mrs. Neal's office. Mrs. Neal motioned for me to sit while she finished recording notes into her tape recorder. I tried not to stare at her, for fear she would think I was eavesdropping on the conversation, even though she didn't seem to care.

"His I.Q. is very low, and he shows signs of depression, talking about suicide regularly and taking a great interest in horrible satanic rock bands such as Led Zeppelin and this Oz Osbourne or whoever he is. Perhaps most telling is that his favorite color is black."

She flipped her wrist back, moving the small microphone away from her thin peach colored lips. I hazarded a glance at her and noticed she was full of color—glittery gray-blue eye shadow covered her enormous eyelids while two streaks of rust colored blush disappeared into her temples and the hornet's nest that was her dyed reddish brown hair. She sat frozen in thought, while her free hand wandered to various parts of her anatomy and surreptitiously scratched. She started with her neck and worked her way down until her hand disappeared and I could only guess what she was scratching.

Unable to conjure any further insights to the mystery student's personality, Mrs. Neal ended her notes with a resounding, "In conclusion, he's not very bright," and dropped the microphone.

Her eyes immediately focused on me, as if she hadn't realized I'd just been privy to the entire confidential file of a fellow student.

"Hello, Katie, we're going to play a game. You like games, don't you?" She stroked her jaw, forming her mouth into a smile.

"Yeah, sure."

"I'm going to show you some pictures and you say whatever comes into your mind. Remember, there are no wrong answers."

Sure. There was always a right answer.

I nodded and she held up a portrait of an older black woman in a blue dress. "Now what do you think of her?"

"Who is she?"

Mrs. Neal quickly read the back of the picture. "This is Harriet Tubman."

"Do I know her?"

Mrs. Neal chuckled. "No, Katie. She lived a long time ago."

"Oh."

"So what do you think of her?"

I shrugged my shoulders. I didn't know what she wanted me to say. "It's a nice picture."

Mrs. Neal frowned. Wrong answer. She groped her right breast before setting Harriet aside and picking up the next picture. This one was a photograph of a boy wearing ragged overalls. Anticipating my first question she said, "This is Booker T. Washington."

"Is he famous?"

"Oh, yes."

"What did he do?"

Mrs. Neal gasped, searching for an answer. "I'm not really sure, but he was very important. Now, what is your reaction to Mr. Washington?"

I looked closely at the picture. "His mother needs to buy him some new clothes." She frowned again. I wasn't doing too well with the answers. The last picture was an oil portrait.

"I know who that is," I said excitedly, leaning forward in my chair. "That's Martin Luther King." I was scoring points now.

"Very good, Katie. Can you tell me anything else about Dr. King?"

"Um, my dad said he worked for civil rights and he believed you shouldn't hit people to get your way. That's why we put the bugs in Athena's desk," I added quickly. Maybe if I told her about Athena, I'd get out of there faster.

Mrs. Neal reached for her tablet and pen. "Explain what you mean, dear."

"Well, my dad told me not to hit people anymore. He said I should think of other ways to show people I'm mad at them."

"And you were mad at Athena?"

"Yeah. She was mean to Angus. So we decided to get her. Instead of beating her up, we put the bugs in her desk." Mrs. Neal fiddled with her pen, while her left hand slid down between her legs.

She raised her eyes slyly. "Tell me, Katie, if you could, would you like to own a slave?"

I shifted in my chair. "What for?"

"Well, to do things for you."

"You mean my slave would have to do whatever I said?"

"Yes." Her eyes brightened.

"Sure." I thought about having someone else to clean my room and eat my green beans.

"Would you like Athena to be your slave?"

I smiled. Maybe Mrs. Neal wasn't so bad after all. "You bet! I'd make her pick up the dog poop and wash my dad's car and go to C.C.D. for me, too!"

Mrs. Neal couldn't write fast enough. When she looked up from her legal pad, she was beaming. "Would you like anyone else to be your slave?"

"You mean I could have more than one?"

"Certainly."

I calculated how many slaves I would need. I'd give one to A.J., and another to Robby, and one to each of my parents. But then, I probably should give my mom two since she had a whole bunch of housework to do. "I'll take six," I said decisively.

Again, Mrs. Neal's hand raced across the page. "Now, who else would you like to be your slave?"

I shrugged my shoulders and glanced at the clock. It was 11:30 and time for lunch. My stomach rumbled.

"Would you like Dr. King to be your slave?"

I blinked. "My dad told me he's dead."

Her face flushed. "I know, dear. But if he were alive, would you want him for a slave?"

I shook my head. "Nah, he'd have too many important things to do."

"What if he didn't have anything else to do? Would you want him then?"

I sighed. "If he weren't dead and if he didn't have anything to do, then sure. He could come over and be my slave." Maybe Dr. King could help dad clean out the garage.

She scribbled some more. "Now Katie, I only have a few more questions. Tell me, if you could spend the day playing with dollies—"

"I don't have any dollies," I quickly stated.

She took a deep breath. "I see. Well, if you did have some dollies, would you rather play tea party with them or build a fort outside?"

At the mention of the words *tea party* my face soured.

Mrs. Neal shook her head. "Don't bother answering that, Katie. I think I already know the answer." She leaned back in the large leather office chair, her arms across her breasts. "I only have one more question for you, Katie. What would you think about wearing pretty sundresses every day of the year?"

My eyes narrowed as I gripped the arms of the chair and said, "I'd rather eat the bugs in Athena's desk."

Mrs. Neal nearly fell backward but she quickly recovered and returned to her notes. "Well, I think that's all for today. Why don't you go to lunch?"

I didn't budge from my chair. "When do I get my slaves?"

"What?"

"Well, you said I could have six slaves. When do I get them?"

Mrs. Neal kept writing. "You don't get them, dear. Slavery is illegal. We were just pretending."

All those dumb questions for a pretend game! At lunch I told A.J. about Dr. Neal's stupid questions. A.J. would see her the next day, so I told her not to take any slaves because Mrs. Neal was just joking and there was no way Athena would really come to her house and work for her.

That afternoon I found myself sitting outside Mrs. Neal's office while she and my parents huddled for an emergency conference. In her haste to inform my parents of my terrible plight, Mrs. Neal had not securely shut her door. I let my foot slowly push the door inward, opening it just enough to hear the conversation.

"Mr. and Mrs. Mitchell," she began, "I am very worried about your daughter."

"Why?" my father asked. "You've met with her once."

"Yes, and in that meeting it became clear to me that your daughter harbors ill will toward people of other ethnicities and she also has issues with her own sexuality."

"That's a lot to conclude after only one twenty-minute conference," my mother said, her voice rising defensively.

"Well, your daughter made it very clear that she feels superior to Athena Witherspoon because the girl is black and when I questioned her about feminine activities, she demonstrated a genuine dislike for all things associated with girlhood."

"Wait, wait," my father interrupted. "I'm with you on the girlhood part. Katie is a tomboy through and through, and my guess is that she'll probably grow out of it as she gets older and starts to show an interest in boys. But my daughter is not prejudiced against anyone. She and her friends pulled that prank because Athena Witherspoon was bullying Angus. If anything, she stood up to a bully and maybe Athena will think twice before she calls people names."

"It doesn't matter that Athena was black," my mother added. "Katie would have stood up for a friend against anyone, regardless of his or her color. That's the way we've raised her, to stand up for her rights and the rights of others."

Mrs. Neal chuckled. "I take it you two are a couple of activists or anti-war sympathizers?"

I could just picture my father bristling at Mrs. Neal's jab. "And what's that supposed to mean?"

"I'm just saying that you've taught Katie to be an inciter, someone who will not show respect for authority."

"Our daughter shows respect for authority but she will also question that authority as well, especially when others are being wronged!" My mother's voice carried out into the hallway and the secretary looked up from her typewriter, assessing the situation, observing me leaning toward the opened door, straining to hear what was said. She grimaced, rose from her chair and shut the door, glaring at me in the process.

I couldn't make out the rest of the conversation, but it wasn't pleasant and it didn't last much longer. My parents stormed out of the office, my father taking my hand and leading me to the parking lot. When we'd all climbed into the station wagon, he turned to face me.

"Did you put those bugs in Athena's desk because she was mean to Angus?"

"Yes."

"Would you have done it to a little white girl?"

"I would have done it to anybody who was mean! Don't you want me standing up for other people?" I asked, my indignation growing. I crossed my arms and glared at my father.

He stared at me seriously but then a slight grin spread across his face. He nodded and my mother turned to me. "Katie, what would you think about wearing a dress to school once a week?"

My mouth dropped open, but my mother raised a hand, already anticipating my response. "Honey, it's just that you're getting to the age where boys might start noticing you and you'll feel embarrassed if you don't look like a girl."

I shook my head and had no response. She was trying to tell me something but I couldn't process it.

"You do want boys to notice you someday, don't you, Katie?"

The loaded question triggered several emotions at once—betrayal, anxiety and shame. I had started to notice other *girls* but I only played with boys as friends and until that moment, I thought those feelings were acceptable. Everything suddenly seemed wrong and all I could do was nod.

Satisfied, my mother faced forward, watching the road ahead, unaware that a door had closed between us.

April 12, 1976

Dear Sister,

Ah, April! My month. The time of year when all of the blooming idiots come out of the woodwork. Nestor came by the other night. It's time for us to organize the annual Easter Beer Hunt. We have held it every year since I first hit Tempe. Only our friend Jim, Nestor and I seem to show up, but that's all right. All the more Easter for us.

Spring always drives me nuts. There is a part of my personality with which you may not be too familiar. I am very big on flower watching. I don't know the names of any of the flowers, so I make up my own names. For instance, there is the Popcorn Bush, the Wretched Gismo, the Flaming Asshole (named in honor of an old friend), the Night Blooming Alcoholic and Frenzied Paper Plant.

I should also tell you that there are certain rules to flower watching. First, you don't pick it. You just watch it. And second, you must respect its integrity. Nestor even gives his flowers the right to vote.

Last week I was watching Let's Make a Deal when the doorbell rang. And what to my wondering eyes should appear but a pretty young thing wearing a Jerry Ford button in her lapel. She was a pollster, and on her other lapel was what I would call a Jesusyourglorious flower. The first I had seen this year! I invited her in and ran down to the basement to get my magnifying glass. Now, let's see, this was about ten in the morning, which means I had already swallowed the better part of a half gallon of Gold Seal Blended Scotch Whiskey (which accounts in part for my watching Let's Make a Deal). She demurely sat on the divan and pulled out some forms.

"Now then, sir. Are you a registered voter?"

"Can I look at your Jesusyourglorious flower?"

"I beg your pardon?"

"Can I sit on your chest and look at your flower? It won't take a minute."

I have never seen a woman bolt for a door faster. Oh well, I have never had much of a way with women. If I looked like Robert Redford she would probably have let me look at her flower. And everything else.

Jerry Ford just lost another vote.

On another governmental note, I am in trouble with the income tax people. Last year I told them that I had sixteen children and three wives. I also said that I was a Mormon elder. The IRS has no sense of humor at all. There is a scant chance that I will go to jail. At least a penitentiary would give me more to write about than a movie theatre could afford.

Pray for me,
Charles

DYKE

Every neighborhood has a great secret spot, a place where the most sensitive and important middle school issues can be shared. In my neighborhood that spot was in A.J.'s backyard. A.J.'s house sat far off the edge of a cul-de-sac, away from the street. A long dirt path led to the only two-story house in the neighborhood, an oddity, but not as odd as A.J.'s parents. Her backyard bordered the canal, a row of trees and thick shrubbery concealing every inch of the yard and the small greenhouse that grew a leafy plant, which I couldn't recognize but A.J. referred to as MJ. I had never heard of people naming their plants, but since A.J. didn't have a dog, I imagined a plant could be a substitute.

Rarely did we allow anyone else into the inner sanctum, especially since A.J.'s parents were very secretive, but once in a while we made an exception when there was good gossip to hear. And on this day, Beryl Sinks, class outcast, had been cornered by the school bully, Kelly MacGuire, and publicly called a FAGGOT. A.J. and I wanted details, so we went to our school's pint-size tabloid reporter, fellow classmate, Tammy Rivers.

Tammy possessed an uncanny intuition and insight, combined with an incredible ability to read lips and hear the quietest conversations from across the bustling cafeteria. Tammy knew all the gossip and gained most of her dirty laundry from her PTA vice president/mother Madeline Rivers. Since my mother was the PTA president, I knew Mrs. Rivers very well. I could always tell when she was about to dish some dirt because she would lower her voice, whisper to my mother and let her right hand rest over her heart, as if to swear she was telling the truth. My mother would usually cut her off in mid-sentence, having no desire to hear gossip.

"So what happened with Beryl and Kelly?" A.J. asked as she threw a dirt clod into the dry canal beneath us.

Tammy situated herself on the lawn chair we'd dragged down from the patio just for her. "Well, you know Kelly has always hated Beryl because he's so weird. Well, this afternoon, at one-o-eight p.m., Beryl was standing at the drinking fountain, when Kelly tried to cut in line. Well, Beryl wouldn't move. He looked Kelly straight in the eye and said no."

Tammy stood up, making the most of her tale. "I don't know why Kelly didn't just pound him into the ground but he didn't. He just looked at him, called him a faggot and walked away. Well, Mrs. Driggs overheard the whole thing, called Principal Counts and Kelly was told never to say the word again."

A.J. snorted. "Why didn't Kelly beat him up?"

As much as I liked A.J., her warped admiration for Kelly MacGuire caused a rift in our friendship.

"I heard," Tammy whispered, "that the reason Kelly chickened out was because Beryl almost showed Kelly his *left* hand."

"No shit!" I exclaimed.

This was serious stuff. Beryl Sinks's left hand was the school mystery. No one had ever seen it. He wore a jean jacket year round, even in the dripping heat of May. Rumors circulated that he really didn't have a hand, only a stump. Others believed it was covered with infectious warts. Regardless of the truth, Beryl was an urban legend and left alone, totally alone.

A.J. heaved another clod. "I wish he would have beaten the crap out of that little faggot. Beryl makes me nervous."

"Beryl's okay," I argued. "He's just different."

A.J. scowled. "He's a queer, that's what he is. Wearing his hair in a ponytail and you know he always wears those girly jeans."

"He's not the only queer at school," Tammy quickly added, attempting to draw the conversation back to herself. She pulled her legs up underneath her, posing like a content cat. "My mom says Miss Jones is a dyke."

"What's a dyke?" I asked, momentarily forgetting that ignorance was not cool.

"A dyke is a woman who wants to be a guy because she likes women." A.J. arched her eyebrows when she said *likes*.

I rolled my eyes. "You're so full of shit, A.J."

"I'm telling you, Katie, it's the truth. Dykes are women who want to kiss other women."

Now personally I couldn't see anything wrong with that but up until this moment, I'd thought all the dikes were in Holland. The whole discussion puzzled me because I couldn't imagine Miss Jones ever being a guy. She was just too cute. In the morning she'd pull up in her little red Mustang convertible just as I was crossing the parking lot (always a planned coincidence). She'd wave and I'd wave back, only to be hit by that old elevator feeling. I'd stop and wait for her so we could walk the rest of the way together. She always wore white shorts and a T-shirt, even in winter. She'd smile at me, her blonde ponytail bobbing up and down as she walked. I had to try very hard not to stare at her legs, legs that fascinated me because each individual muscle flexed with every step. She was a goddess.

"All I know," Tammy continued, "is that Miss Jones is living with a woman and my mom says only dykes live like that."

"I think you're both full of it," I announced.

"Geez, Katie," A.J. exclaimed, "If Tammy says it's true, then you know it is."

"Yeah, right. This is just like when you told me I'd start to bleed when I turned eleven and it didn't happen until I was twelve!"

"Well, you're just defective," A.J. joked. I pounced on her and we both rolled down the canal bank, the discussion forgotten for the afternoon.

Madeline Rivers, however, as PTA vice president and wife of a minister, wasn't as forgetful. Between Tammy and her mother, word spread from parent to parent, and by the end of the month, all of the kids at school were talking about Miss Jones, having learned second, third or fourth hand that she was a "dyke." My parents didn't seem to care.

"Mom, what's a dyke?" I asked during dinner one night.

My parents glanced at each other and my mother chewed her food slowly, stalling to process her answer. She daintily patted the sides of her lips before she looked at me. "Katie, the first thing you need to know is that the word dyke is offensive and crude. The correct term is lesbian or homosexual and I do not want to hear you say that word again, even if others do." She smiled and I knew I wasn't in trouble. "A lesbian is a woman who is attracted to another female."

"So they don't like men?"

"It's not that they don't like men," my dad said. "But they don't want to get married to them, like me and your mom."

My face flushed thinking of Kimmie Lancaster. She was the only person I'd ever wanted to marry, at least so far. "Is it bad to be a lesbian?" I asked, my voice squeaking out the question.

Both of my parents shook their heads and my younger siblings imitated their emphatic reactions. "Well, honey, it's another way to live. Now, our religion says that it's a sin but what other people do is not our business," my mother answered. She put her hand on my shoulder and gave it a squeeze. "I know how much you like Miss Jones and I know some very narrow-minded people are saying some very mean things about her. You just keep doing well in her class and letting her know you think she's a great teacher."

"She is a great teacher," I agreed.

Later that evening, the doorbell rang after I went to bed. I crept down the stairs to see who had arrived since no one visited my parents after eight thirty on a school night. From around the corner I could see my mother leading the Wright Elementary PTA board into the living room.

It was Madeline Rivers, my mother's second-in-command, who chose to speak for the group. "Barbara, we are very concerned that you are blocking our efforts to have a forum about Miss Jones. Don't you think the parents have a right to know about the kind of woman who is teaching our children?"

My mother raised her chin and glared at Madeline. "And exactly what kind of woman do you find Miss Jones to be?" she asked.

Madeline cleared her throat and shifted uncomfortably on the sofa. "You know as well as I do what people are saying. Miss Jones does not lead a normal life."

My mother started to laugh. "Normal? And what defines normal?"

"You know what I'm saying!" Madeline hissed. "Miss Jones has an unnatural lifestyle, one that is condemned by the Bible and could morally corrupt our children. Don't you worry about her influence over Katie?"

"Not at all. Cindy Jones has done nothing but encourage Katie and all of the other children to be physically fit and have positive attitudes about sports and competition. She is one of the finest teachers I have ever met."

Madeline waved a finger at my mother. "There! You said it! She does have influence and that's what we're all very concerned about, the control she has over our children. She's a teacher, and she molds the views of our kids. There's no way I want her turning my little Tammy into a dyke!"

My mother looked at the three women. When she spoke, her voice was controlled and steady. "I doubt very seriously that Tammy will ever become a homosexual. I am going to ask all of you to leave now. I will not tolerate prejudice and bigotry in my home, especially when it is directed at someone I admire. As the PTA president, I refuse to conduct a forum, so if you want that, Madeline, you'll have to go to Principal Counts."

She stood and walked to the door while they gathered their coats. Madeline Rivers turned to my mother before she exited. "This isn't over, Barbara. Perhaps you aren't the right person to be PTA president. Maybe you should step down."

My mother leaned very close to her vice president. "Let's be very clear. I will never resign. If you want me gone, you'll have to get the majority of the membership to throw me out, because I'm not going anywhere." With those words, my mother practically shoved the door closed on Mrs. Rivers. She stood there for a few seconds, regaining her composure, trying to get her hands to stop shaking.

Without looking up the stairs, I heard her say, "Go to bed now, Katie, honey."

The gossip continued but Miss Jones didn't seem to notice what was going on behind her back. She always smiled and offered words of encouragement, even to Kelly MacGuire. He'd throw a good pass or make a hard shot during phys ed and Miss Jones would be screaming, "Way to go, Kelly!"

If only she'd known. Every day at lunch Kelly would spout a litany of hatred. "I know all about queers and faggots," he claimed. "My daddy lost his job to a queer. They're immoral and they're Communists, because no red, white and blue American man would ever want to kiss another man. And lezzies are the worst because if all the women wanted to be with other women, then there wouldn't be any more babies and eventually people would die out."

I watched the kids around me, particularly A.J., whose dark ponytail nodded in fierce agreement. I glanced at A.J., her baseball cap firmly on her head, wearing her usual jeans and T-shirt. We were so much alike that I couldn't help wondering if she'd ever had feelings like I did.

I sat there with the others, listening to Kelly, feeling horrible for Miss Jones. I wanted to defend her but I couldn't. First, I wasn't stupid. Kelly MacGuire could kill me. Second, a small part of me, a very small part, wondered if he wasn't right. Every time I overheard Kelly's booming voice talking about girls kissing, I imagined my lips kissing Marcia Brady, my latest crush. Goose pimples rose on my forearms but then a wave of shame would evaporate them.

The older I grew, the more I realized that my feelings for girls were unusual. You never saw two women kissing each other on TV. The song my dad sang in the shower was called "When a *Man* Loves a *Woman*." Dudley Doo Right rescued Nell. Mickey Mouse loved Minnie Mouse. Mary had Joseph and my mom had my dad. Every picture, advertisement, book, toy and movie depicted a family as a father, a mother and assorted children. Men went with women—or did they?

The adults didn't notice their bigotry had infested most of their children. They were too busy lobbying Principal Counts to do something about Miss Jones who had brought her roommate Dawn to the spring play, causing a huge flurry of activity during intermission. I actually got to meet Dawn because my parents were the only adults who made an effort to talk with her and Miss Jones. Everyone else either ignored them or politely nodded and moved away quickly.

Miss Jones would say nothing. She neither admitted nor denied the accusations. She just kept doing her job and ignored the gossip and talk. Things died down for a while. For us kids the luster and interest of hate waned by the end of April. We'd re-focused our emotions on something really important, the upcoming Little League season. So when something did happen three weeks before the end of school, we were all surprised.

As Tammy Rivers would later report, it was at 10:17, during the morning recess kickball game when Kelly MacGuire kicked a foul ball that skidded into the fence and landed at the feet of Beryl Sinks. It is unknown to this day whether what happened next was deliberate or accidental: Beryl kicked the ball deep into the outfield.

Kelly stormed over to Beryl, pushing anyone aside who tried to intercede. Beryl took three steps away from the fence, his left hand still confined to his jacket pocket. Kelly walked right into Beryl and shoved him against the fence.

"What the hell do you think you're doing, faggot?"

"Don't ever call me that again," Beryl replied, in a voice Tammy described as "maniacal."

"Call you what? Faggot? Is that the word I'm not supposed to call you, faggot?" Kelly laughed and most of the surrounding crowd joined in. Kelly turned to acknowledge their appreciation and that's when it happened. To the gasps of the crowd, Beryl Sinks slid his left hand from his jacket. Onlookers said it was huge, totally out of proportion with the rest of his arm. His fingers were long and bony, like barrels of a .357 Magnum. They quickly curled and when Kelly MacGuire jerked around to see what had caught the crowd's attention, Beryl Sinks drove that steel fist into Kelly's large proboscis (Tammy's word for nose.)

The blow lifted Kelly's one hundred-fifty pound frame off the ground momentarily, until he fell into an unconscious heap. Beryl's fist quickly disappeared back into the depths of his jacket. He leaned over the crumpled Kelly and said, "I told you not to call me that," and walked away.

Despite the appearance of Beryl's legendary left hand, the whole incident probably wouldn't have been recorded in the annals of Wright Elementary history if it hadn't been for the punishment handed out to the boys. Kelly received a day's detention for taunting Beryl and Beryl got a three-day suspension. Most of us were surprised, having seen or experienced Kelly's bullying firsthand.

Miss Jones was outraged.

After hearing about Beryl's suspension through the school grapevine, she roared into Principal Count's office and according to Tammy, who just happened to be there on an errand, the conversation went something like this:

Miss Jones: John, what the hell do you mean by giving Kelly MacGuire a one-day detention?

Principal Counts: Cindy, don't you have a class now?

Miss J: Len Moore is covering for me and don't change the subject. How can you give Beryl Sinks a three-day suspension when all he did was defend himself after enduring six months of taunting insults?

Principal C: The boy assaulted another student (emphasis on assaulted).

Miss J: He never would have if Kelly had left him alone!

Principal C: But he did! And he has no right to punch another student in the nose.

Miss J: But Kelly has the right to call Beryl a faggot?

Principal C: I never said that. There's a difference, though, between verbal abuse and physical abuse.

Miss J: Oh, there is?

Principal C: Most definitely. Students call each other names all the time. We'd never have any kids in school if I suspended them each time they cut somebody down.

Miss J: This is different.

Principal C: I don't think it is but I do think you're just a little more sensitive because of the nature of Kelly's prejudice.

Miss J: What the hell does that mean?

Principal C: It means that it doesn't surprise me that you're a little sensitive to Beryl's situation.

Miss J: In other words, all us faggots stick together?

Principal C: You're putting words in my mouth, Cindy.

Miss J: And you're putting labels on me.

(At this point, Miss Jones threw open the principal's door and left with Principal Counts following her. She got as far as the ditto machine before whirling around and making the following speech in front of the whole office):

How dare you, *(to administrative staff)* or any of you, make assumptions about my life. You know nothing about me. I know what you all think and I don't care. It's none of your damn business who I date, who I sleep with or who I marry. I'm tired of being whispered about and pointed at. Think whatever you want. What none of you know is that there are several gay teachers at this school. You'll probably spend the rest of the night trying to figure out who they are. *(To Principal Counts):* And as for you, John, you're a prejudiced bigot who lets the parents lead you around on a leash.

Ms. Jones then grabbed a ditto master and wrote "I QUIT!" She thrust it in Principal Counts' face before storming out of the office.

Miss Jones was absent for the next week, placed on administrative leave, which was a nice way of getting rid of someone temporarily until you knew what you wanted to do with them permanently. Everybody knew what had happened between her and Principal Counts. They knew about it but they spent more time whispering about potential gay teachers. Miss Jones proved to be a prophet and the Beryl-Kelly fight and aftermath were already forgotten.

I didn't think I'd ever see Miss Jones again but that Saturday night she turned up in my living room. I'd gone downstairs to get a drink of water and saw her in the dining room with my mother, a box of Kleenex between them. I quickly went back upstairs, no longer needing the water. I didn't even try to listen at the stairs. I'd had my fill of gossip.

On Monday Principal Counts announced on the P.A. that Miss Jones had decided to resign. No reason was given.

Beryl served his suspension and for the rest of the year spent his recesses leaning against the back fence, his left hand in his pocket. The older kids moved their daily kickball game to the front field and Kelly MacGuire, whose nose had been broken in two places, became one of the quietest students in the whole school (partly because it hurt to talk for the first two weeks).

Miss Jones kept in touch with my mother. As a former teacher and current parent, mom wrote a shining recommendation, and Miss Jones found a job in a private school. Two years later, I attended Miss Jones's wedding to a minor league baseball player. It was there I met her former roommate and the roommate's "life partner."

No one from Wright Elementary was invited to the wedding except my parents and me. I couldn't understand why Miss Jones had suffered so unnecessarily. For days after the wedding I pondered Miss Jones's behavior and it didn't make sense. When I finally asked my mother why Miss Jones hadn't denied the rumors, why she hadn't stayed and fought, why she'd quit, my mother's response was simple.

"Because, Katie, she shouldn't have to."

Switching Partners

"How much time we got?" A.J. asked.

I checked my watch. "About twenty minutes before *Grease.*"

A.J. hopped on the vanity, her back against the mirror. Several women entered the bathroom and some occasionally stopped to primp, but none seemed to care that we were just sitting there, hiding out. We were theater hoppers, small-time criminals biding time until the next movie started. One ticket bought us a day of films, popcorn and neck strain. The fact that theater switching was illegal didn't deter us from seeing *Animal House* fifteen times in three weekends.

"Hey, are you going to the dance with Robby?"

"No. He's decided Beth Simms is a better kisser."

"Robby kisses you?"

I sighed. "He used to. It's no big deal. He smashes his lips against mine and rolls his tongue around in my mouth."

"Sounds disgusting."

"It is."

"If you don't like it, why do you do it?"

I shrugged my shoulders. I really wasn't attracted to any of the boys at school but the social implications of relationships and dating were severe for the President of the Student Council. It was crucial to have a boyfriend, even if he dated other people. In grade school, association overrode monogamy.

I volleyed the question back. "Are you gonna go?"

She shook her head. "In the first place, I'm not wearing no damn dress. And second, I hate those streamers they always hang. It looks like a birthday party for a five-year-old. And I'm not gonna stand against the wall like Freda Mullin, waiting for some boy to ask me to dance."

An idea occurred to me. "Hey, A.J., why don't you and I go together? You could be my date."

"What? I'm not a homo, Kate."

"It wouldn't be a real date. It's not like we'll go to the canal bank after the dance and neck. It'd just be like two friends going out."

A.J. mulled this over and nodded.

I didn't think twice about asking A.J. because I wasn't interested in her. Now, if it were Beth Simms, Robby's date, then that would be different. Beth and I had been acquaintances since first grade but until this year, I'd never really noticed her until Robby's birthday party that summer. She looked fabulous in a swimsuit. Now, every time I got near Beth my throat went dry, that old elevator feeling came back and I was reduced to a blithering idiot.

Friday night came and my dad drove A.J. and me to the dance. The dance committee had tacked up a few streamers, attempting to transform the cafeteria into a teenage disco. Fat chance. A.J. was right. It looked like a kiddie party.

Music blared from the small hi-fi, but no one was dancing. All of the boys sat against the east wall, facing the girls on the west, a bunch of lemmings waiting for their leaders to take charge. As Elton John's "Island Girl" began, two courageous boys walked across the great divide and motioned to their established girlfriends. Soon most everyone was bopping to the music, including A.J. and me. Seeing two girls dancing, several of the wallflowers joined us and by the end of the song, our couple had become a group. We all danced the next five songs until a slow Chicago song started. A.J. and I went for punch.

Robby leaned against the refreshment table, his right arm slung over Beth's shoulder. "Don't have a date, huh, Kate?"

"Yes, I do. I'm with A.J."

Robby laughed. "A.J. can't be your date. She's a girl!"

"So what? I can date anyone I want to."

"Any guy. You can't date girls. It's wrong." Robby removed his arm from Beth, so he could face off against me.

"Who says it's wrong?" We all looked at Beth, who stood there with her hands on her hips.

Robby swallowed hard. "Everybody," he said weakly.

"Girls can do anything they want, Robby Wentworth. Besides, I think Kate would be a better date than you. We've been here an hour and you haven't asked me to dance once."

"I don't like to dance," Robby protested.

"But I do!" Beth turned to me. "Kate, would you dance with me?"

I nearly spilled my punch. "But it's a slow dance," I said.

"I don't care."

Robby was furious. A.J. was laughing. My heart was pounding. "Okay."

We went to the center of the dance floor and bear-hugged as the BeeGees' falsetto voices filled the room. I felt the slow rise and fall of Beth's chest against the bass drum of my heart.

This was absolutely unbelievable. We danced in circles but I was numb and totally unaware of anything except her strawberry scented hair. The BeeGees faded away and our bodies separated.

"That was fun," she said.

"Yeah, it was," I mumbled.

"I think I'm going to ask Nancy Holden to dance next." Beth advanced to Nancy who laughed but agreed to ditch her date and join Beth on the floor. Robby watched from the refreshment table, shaking his head and stamping his feet.

A.J. and I went back onto the floor and started to move to "Boogie Fever." By the end of the song, Nancy and Beth had boogied over to us and we formed a quartet for the next three songs. The longer we danced, the more girls joined us. If the boys didn't want to dance, that was just fine. We could have more fun with each other and that included slow dancing.

Hall and Oates's "Sara Smile" began and the girls partnered up. A.J. would have nothing to do with slow dancing, so Beth asked me.

If I were going to die young, I prayed a lightning bolt would strike me down and I would fry in Beth's arms. She hugged me tightly and my whole body tingled.

"What do you think the boys are thinking?" she whispered.

"I'll bet they're pretty pissed off."

She laughed and touched her forehead against mine. If we were any closer, we'd be kissing. "You know what?"

"What?"

"I don't care," she smiled, exposing years of orthodontia. Her lips were perfect and I imagined them touching mine. We bear hugged for the rest of the song and only let go of each other when the next song began. Beth smiled at me and I started to laugh, hoping she would see I was totally cool with our dance, when in fact my body was experiencing chemical reactions I had never known.

The girls ostracized the boys for the rest of the night and danced with each other. The boys stayed against their wall, talking and acting cool. If our behavior bothered them, they certainly weren't going to show it.

The adult chaperones were a different matter. They must have said something to Principal Counts because on the following Monday, he mentioned the dance on the morning announcements.

"Good morning, students," he warbled into the microphone. "I hope you all had a pleasant weekend. I would like to thank the dance committee for the lovely job they did last Friday night.

"And while we're on the subject of dances, I noticed something which disturbed me. Halfway through the evening, the boys were no longer dancing. It seemed all of you young ladies decided to exclude the gentleman from the festivities and dance with each other instead.

"This is inappropriate for two reasons. First, it's not fair to exclude anyone and clearly the boys were being left out. Second, it just isn't right." He coughed and cleared his throat. "From now on, all couples on the dance floor will be boy-girl."

At lunch, A.J. and I sat next to Beth and Robby. Robby poked at his food in silence, still angry with the three of us and the female population in general. Beth, however, was very talkative.

"Kate, can you believe Principal Counts? I mean, all we did was dance together!" She polished off her milk and took a bite of her apple. "He makes it sound like we committed a crime or something. We didn't do anything wrong."

Robby set down his fork. "Yeah, you did. You left us all sitting there like a bunch of jerks."

"You guys never want to dance."

"Maybe I would have later, if I'd known you girls were going to dance together. You looked really stupid."

"We did not!" I argued. There was no way Robby was going to trample one of the most significant moments in my life.

"You did too! It isn't natural for girls to dance with girls, Kate. Everybody knows that!"

Beth stood up. "God, it was no big deal, Robby!" Beth turned to me. "Kate, I had a wonderful time at the dance, thanks to you." She shot a glare at Robby before leaning over the table in front of me. I tried not to stare at Beth's developing breasts, nor squish the fruit pie in my hand.

"There's something I forgot to give you Friday night."

"What?" I whispered.

She kissed me square on the lips and walked away. Robby stormed off and A.J. laughed. I dropped my pie into my lap.

November 18, 1978

Dearest Sister Mine,

I am happy to report that I have left my position as Portofino's premiere projectionist and taken a job as a cameraman at KJTP, Tucson's own independent TV station. I'm sure my outstanding resume, which was written that morning on a cocktail napkin, combined with my glowing personality, secured me the position. It probably helped too that my friend Nestor is sleeping with the boss's daughter.

I must also tell you that I was momentarily fired the first day of my employment, and I am now on vacation after only three days of work. My boss, Horace Rothman, insists that it doesn't have to do with the FCC boys coming to town for their annual inspection. Apparently the boys from DC heard something about my, well, indiscretion on the first day.

What happened was actually quite innocent. We were showing the New Mickey Mouse Club and the director called for a sixty second fill film. My film man was busy, so I picked the film and put it up. It was a public service announcement dealing with examination of the female breast for cancer. I am of the opinion that women should be aware of such things. Even very young women who don't yet have breasts. So what if it was explicit? Don't mothers want their daughters to know about such things?

Apparently many of the homemakers in the greater Tucson area do not share my views or the conservative Mormon who owns the station.

As for life away from work, I am planning a driving trip with Nestor over to San Diego for a funeral. Seems a biker friend of his had an unfortunate meeting with a truck on I-10. It should be quite the affair, since the friend's last name was O'Shaunnessy.

It is a well-known fact that only the Irish and the Chinese know how to hold a funeral. Irish women say enough prayers and light enough candles to guarantee a Pharaoh a niche in Christ's heaven, and it's rare that a bad word is ever spoken of the deceased, at least while the wake is still going on. I find it strange that among all the people of Europe, it is the Irish alone who have discovered the efficacy of the wake. All others pale beside it. A funeral says, "We are sorry he is gone." A wake says, "We are glad he was here."

Give my love to everyone. Nestor and I are going out tonight to search for our lost youth. He's certain he knows where he left it.

Your still employed brother,
Charles

Present Day

My parents' storage unit hasn't been opened in ten years since they decided that an extra seven-by-eight-foot room would be just enough space for all of the memorabilia, trinkets and antiques that couldn't fit in the house but were, in fact, the cornerstones of family history. No one can remember what is actually stored inside—the past sheds its skin daily for the present and the ever arriving future.

We meet on a Saturday morning, my father, my brother, myself and Sarah, who, as a good wife, participates in such family labors. Ironically it is my sister, Karen, who is absent, the one child who moved away and the one who possesses the greatest knowledge of family history. It will be difficult to recognize the significance of the seemingly meaningless articles we come across as we open each box and decide whether it is worthy to trek back to my parents' house or if it belongs in Sarah's and my SUV, ready to go to Goodwill.

The entire purpose of the visit is not lost on anyone as my father works the combination of the padlock. It is my mother's absence that has allowed my father to free himself of the monthly storage bill, turning her sewing room into a larger, low-cost version of the cubicle they now rent. My brother slides the metal accordion door up, revealing the map of our family's heritage in boxes and containers that stretch from the floor to the ceiling.

"That's a lot of stuff," Sarah says under her breath and the entire task seems very daunting.

"Let's just start," I exclaim with a groan as I pick up a heavy box and set it on a cart. When I open it, I recognize many of my parents' toys from childhood, an old metal bank that belonged to my great-grandfather, a doll from the early 1940s and my father's old fire engine. I marvel at the craftsmanship, the weight of the hardwood and the steel. None of the toys is cheap and they are an antique dealer's dream.

We branch out, each of us opening a box on this warped version of Christmas. A surprise waits in each one and our task is slowed when an amazing or humorous artifact is uncovered and we all must take a moment to share in the find. Tommy locates several photo albums from our grandparents, my father uncovers my mother's wedding gown but it is Sarah, reaching deep into a corner, who discovers my grandparents' old Brownie movie camera, projector and a box of reels.

"Some of these are at least fifty years old," Sarah says, reading the label of the reel carton. "And some of them are of you." She grins at me and I notice the date: 1964. The year I was born. We put the reels aside and continue our quest of sorting, verifying and evaluating. Of course, the giveaway pile is very small, all of us erring on the conservative side of posterity. Hours later, we are dirty and sweaty from the chore, the storage unit empty and all of our precious memories safely returned to my parents' house.

I retrieve the movie camera, projector and reels from the back seat. All of us are eager to see the films, as my father cannot remember any of the content. We thread the projector after many missteps, none of us familiar with this primitive technology. What flashes on to the white wall surprises us instantaneously.

The first image is of my mother, young and vibrant, probably in her mid-twenties. She wears a simple cotton dress, typical of the time, and her hair curls around her heart-shaped face. I lean forward, frustrated at the graininess of the film and the distance that separates my mother from the camera lens. Whoever shot the movie was standing at least fifteen feet away, unaware that viewers would want to see some closeups. My mother gracefully turns toward the camera, her A-line skirt sweeping in the wind.

"Wow, she had a great body," Sarah comments.

I look at my lover, shocked. "That's my mother you're drooling over!"

Sarah only shrugs. "Honey, that woman has a sixteen-inch waist, curves that never end and legs that a dancer would envy. For the Sixties, your mother is hot."

Even Luke cannot believe that he is watching his grandmother. He sees nothing similar between the lady who holds a large chubby baby with a thick tuft of dark hair (me) and the frail invalid he visits once a month. "That's Grammy?" he exclaims, his finger pointing at the screen.

We watch a slightly overweight young man enter the frame, dressed in a white shirt and dark pants. The wind is blowing and the man brushes his shoulder length dark hair out of his eyes. An enormous smile covers his face and he reaches to take me from my mother. "Who's that?" Luke asks, studying the strange man.

"That's Great Uncle Charlie," I tell him. "He was your Grammy's brother. You would have really liked him."

Sarah leans close and whispers, "Wasn't he the first person you came out to?"

I nod. Sarah has heard me tell many of Uncle Charlie's colorful stories and she has read some of his letters. Eventually my father enters the picture and puts his arm around my mother. The three of them wave at the camera, talk to me and chat amongst themselves until the filmmaker, satisfied that he has exhausted the importance of the moment, clicks the camera off. Only a few frames remain, and then the tick-tick sound is heard as the celluloid tail is freed of the projector.

I stare at the white screen and close my eyes. No one speaks or comments as my father turns off the projector and we are left sitting in the darkened room. Luke, the master of levity, pats me on the shoulder.

"Well, Mom, that wasn't a very good movie. It didn't have any special effects and they used a broken camera."

"Why do you think the camera was broken?" I ask.

"Because it didn't have any sound."

We all laugh and Luke grins, pleased that he has amused us. He jumps off the bed and turns on the lights. My brother quickly brings his hand to his face and wipes away the tears that went unnoticed before. He looks over at me and I smile slightly. He tries to smile back and gives a slight nod.

It is the first time I have ever seen my brother cry.

Fresh Meat

I couldn't do it. My intestines twisted into knots while I waited in the darkened auditorium for my turn to perform. My right leg bobbed up and down while I tried to focus my attention to the stage. I pretended to be listening but in fact, my mind was rehearsing my own monologue assignment, which I was certain would vanish the minute I stood in the footlights, an acute bout of stage fright overtaking me—again.

This was the second monologue assignment in Stagecraft I, a drama class for high school freshmen. My first one had proven disastrous, my anxiety so intense that only eight sentences came out of my mouth before I forgot everything else. I was certain that this monologue, which Beth had picked for me from *Who's Afraid of Virginia Woolf*, would be the end of my career in drama and my first "F" in my very short high school career.

Beth reached over and placed a reassuring hand on my spastic knee. Her delicate fingers rested on top of mine and I relaxed. I glanced over at my best friend, the girl who convinced me to enroll in drama rather than physical education. Her eyes remained glued to the stage and James's performance. Our newest friend emoted and fell to his knees, hands clenched in fists, as his character, Creon, reached his catharsis. Beth suddenly removed her hand from mine to applaud and I joined her, still reciting my lines over and over in my head.

James bopped off the stage and landed in the chair next to me. I smiled at him and Beth reached over me to give James a high five.

"Kate Mitchell, you're next," Mr. Mayes called from somewhere behind us.

Beth squeezed my knee and smiled, reminding me why I had forsaken PE and sports for the girl who was my secret desire.

"Go get 'em, Kate," James called.

I trudged to the stage and wiped my sweaty palms on my designer jeans, the ones Beth convinced me to buy because she said I looked great in them. I squinted toward the seats, unable to see any faces against the glare of the lights from above. I involuntarily crinkled my script, my crutch against total failure.

I took a breath and barreled through the opening lines, words tumbling over each other, like a crowd exiting a building during a fire. My pace only slowed when my memory began to fail, until a dead silence enveloped the auditorium. I opened my mouth, hoping the lines I'd practiced endlessly with Beth in her tree house would magically slip through my lips. Instead I just stood there, mouth agape, looking like a statue. Damn! It was happening again.

When nothing came out, I finally turned to my script, my eyes scanning the words, searching for the next lines. "I've said that, and that, and that," I murmured quietly.

"Kate?" Mr. Mayes called. "That's fine. You can stop there." I nodded, grateful for his compassionate reprieve.

I returned to my seat. "You did great, Kate," Beth gushed. "It was much better than last time."

"She's right," James agreed, giving me a quick kiss on the cheek.

"Don't lie, you guys. I am the worst student in this class."

"That's not true, honey," James said. "Theresa's much worse than you."

I dismissed their comments as pathetic charity and stared at the floor, my head buried in my hands. I pondered whether a schedule change was still possible.

"You all right?" a strange, deep voice asked.

Before I looked up, my nostrils filled with men's cologne. My gaze met the steel gray eyes of Arturo Ortega, senior technical director. My mouth dropped open. Artie never talked to freshmen.

He was always around and we'd all watched him dart in and out of our class on his way to the scene shop, interrupting class to ask Mr. Mayes a question. He never looked at any of us since we were not worthy to know him. Consequently, I'd never seen him this close, and I realized now why so many of the girls drooled over him. He wasn't very tall but well-defined muscles filled out his tight T-shirt. He looked much older than seventeen, a pencil thin mustache covering his upper lip and a small gold hoop earring dangled from his right ear. He wore his jet black hair longer than most of the students, giving him a dangerous, rebellious look.

I nodded slightly in answer to his question and he quickly turned away, heading up the aisle toward Mr. Mayes. Beth looked at me, stunned by the moment. I shrugged my shoulders.

"Kate!" Mr. Mayes shouted.

I jumped at the sound of my name and turned around in my seat. Mr. Mayes was waving for me to join him and Artie.

Gone was the compassionate look from Artie's face, replaced by one of annoyance. "Kate, I'd like you to help Artie from now on during your drama period. He needs someone to work with him on the lights."

I doubted Artie needed help nearly as much as Mr. Mayes needed a break from my acting.

"Sure," I said, glancing at Artie, who fumed quietly.

Artie sighed. "Follow me," he commanded. We went into the scene shop filled with set pieces, props, flats and Artie's beloved lights. "We keep the extra lekos and fresnels here," he said, pointing to two different compartments. "The lighting accessories like gels, top hats and gobos are over here." He opened some large drawers and I glanced inside, not understanding a word he was saying.

He walked to a large open space and spread his arms out. "This is the set design area. Paint is on the shelves and the prop closet is organized alphabetically. Don't mess it up," he threatened.

I spent the rest of the period and many more just following him around, learning what I could when he decided to speak to me, which was an average of five words a day. By the third quarter, Artie's exterior melted as I proved my usefulness. He would occasionally reward me with a grin or a chuckle and once in a great while he would squeeze my shoulder in praise. Working in the theatre department proved enjoyable and it gave me a chance to spend almost every minute of the day with Beth who Mr. Mayes had labeled as the rising ingénue of the department. She had just been cast as the lead of the spring musical, *Once Upon a Mattress*, the first freshman in Valley High history to receive such an honor. She was overjoyed when she found her name at the top of the cast list, throwing her arms around me, hugging me tightly. My whole body tingled as our breasts pressed against each other and her green eyes sparkled into mine.

"I made it!" she exclaimed. "And James is playing my father and you're the assistant stage manager! We're all going to be together!" I nodded, unable to speak, watching her perfect ruby lips form the words.

The play consumed us and we spent endless hours and weekends at the auditorium, two of the few freshmen accepted by the upperclassmen.

"I think Artie likes you," Beth announced on opening night. She was putting on her makeup and I was preparing the props.

My shock was difficult to hide. "What are you talking about? Artie's like a god! He's not interested in anyone and certainly not me."

"Do you like him?" Beth probed. Her expression was serious and I could tell she was trying to read my emotions. My answer mattered to her, but how could I tell her that I really liked *her*? She would freak out and I would lose my best friend.

"I've never even thought about it." And that was the truth. I'd never thought of Artie as a love interest. I'd never thought of any boy that way. "I'm sure you're wrong," I said and quickly left the dressing room.

The play was a huge success and Beth was phenomenal. We were all riding an enormous high on our way to the cast party. Beth, James and I hitched a ride with Artie in his old '72 Nova, all of us recounting the best moments of the show. As we followed the dirt road up to the party house, we could already hear the music. All the lights were on and we heard a huge laugh come from somewhere in the bushes.

"We're here," Artie announced, a sly grin on his face. "You three freshmen have never been to a Drama Party, have you?"

We shook our heads and Artie faced us, his hands crossed over his chest. "Then let me give you some advice. First, don't drink anything but the wine. Tasha loves to make these hallucinogenic drinks that will knock you on your ass. Second, we will inevitably wind up playing Truth or Dare. Be very careful about doing anything with Kyle. Always pick truth, okay?" We nodded. "Finally, whatever happens at a Drama Party *stays* at the Drama Party, got it?"

We agreed and followed Artie into Tasha's enormous home. Her parents must have been gone for the night or they probably wouldn't have approved of the thirty bottles of wine that sat on the dining room table, all purchased with fake ID's on the way over. Artie added his contribution and led us into the living room where the lights were turned down and I could only see silhouettes huddled together, their conversations and laughter competing with the blaring Journey album. The lights were off, only candles glowed and the smell of pot and cigarettes couldn't be camouflaged by the incense burning throughout the house.

"I'll catch you all later," Artie said, joining a group of pot smokers huddled in the giant bay window.

Abandoned, Beth, James and I wandered through the rooms, armed with our own Styrofoam cups of bad wine. Beth held my hand, for which I was grateful and delighted. Although I knew most of the people who nodded at us approvingly as we toured the house, none invited us to join their private conversations and others had no interest in socializing having already found a dark corner for some heavy petting and groping. My heart started to pound as I gazed into the corner of the den and watched one of the female stagehands slide her hand up the skirt of the girl who played Beth's mother. Neither noticed me ogling them, for their mouths and tongues were very preoccupied.

"They're having fun," Beth commented, and she gave my hand a squeeze.

James drifted toward a group of boys and Beth and I found ourselves on the patio, where many people were dancing to leftover disco songs. Two sophomore boys immediately appeared at our sides, determined to monopolize our time and conversation. Too polite to say no, we danced with them. I had finished my second glass of wine and I was definitely lightheaded. I heard myself laugh heartily at my dance partner's unfunny joke and I vowed to stop drinking.

The music abruptly stopped and a voice shouted, "Truth or Dare!"

All of the thespians found their way back into the living room, in various states of inebriation and dress, until we were in a circle. Beth, who was definitely a little drunk, took my hand again and rested her head on my shoulder. I made a note to get her drunk more often.

At the head of the circle, Tasha Delacroix, drama department queen, motioned for quiet. She waited until everyone was silent and the stereo was turned off. Unbelievably, she turned to Beth, James and me.

"I want to welcome our three newest members and allow you the first question."

She gestured with a flourish, giving us the floor. James, ever the bubbly gay man, raised his hand. "I'll go first!" Tasha nodded her assent and James looked around at everyone in the circle, his eyes settling on his own desire, Brad, the handsome junior who always played the male leads.

"Brad, Truth or Dare!"

Brad, well aware of James's affections, smiled. "Truth, James."

Emboldened by the wine, James crawled into the middle of the circle until he was face to face with Brad. "Would you ever consider making out with me?"

The circle erupted in laughter and hoots. Brad's face turned crimson and he blinked. He glanced around at the other faces and took a deep breath. "Yes," he whispered. Brad grabbed James by the shirt collar and pulled him closer until they were kissing.

Everyone applauded as James and Brad remained pressed together for a complete minute.

Tasha clapped her hands together for silence. "All right. We need to move along. You boys can take your romance to another room, preferably the guest room."

James and Brad darted out of the circle and Tasha's eyes turned to Beth.

"Beth, it's your turn."

Beth rubbed her hands and smiled at Tasha, who was her idol. Although Beth was the ingénue, Tasha was the true leading actress and would be heading to New York in the fall for acting school. Beth and I were both in awe of her, although I suspected for different reasons. We admired her incredible stage presence, which to Beth probably meant an incredible ability to emote Shakespeare but to me it was a great ass and a perfect bust.

"Tasha, Truth or Dare."

Tasha, a model of haughtiness, craned her neck and flared her nostrils. "Truth, Beth."

"If you could have any guy in school, who would it be?"

Tasha blinked and sat up. "Mr. Meadows."

We all laughed but Tasha was stone serious.

"You'd go for the principal? Why in God's name would you want him, Tasha?" cried Dallas McBroom, senior sleeze.

"Because he's the only man in the school with any real power."

"Yeah, and he's also fuckin' fifty years old," Dallas retorted.

Tasha's icy stare silenced Dallas. "Age has nothing to do with sex," she responded. "It's my turn. Dallas, since you're being such a prick, I'll pick on you. Truth or Dare."

"Dare," came the playful reply. Dallas embraced Tasha, kissing her on the cheek. "What do you want me to do, baby?"

Tasha wiped her cheek. "I want to see this new tattoo that you've been bragging about."

"Gladly." Dallas jumped up and dropped his pants, sticking his rear end in Tasha's face. "Very nice," she commented. Dallas paraded around the room, showing everyone the beautiful monarch butterfly on his left buttock. We all hooted and cheered at Dallas's performance and his body. Dallas was very well endowed.

He came full circle and once again stuck his butt in front of Tasha. She sat up and bit him right in the butterfly. "Ouch!" Dallas screamed. "What the fuck was that, Tasha?"

"I thought you loved it when people kissed your ass."

We all laughed hysterically, except Dallas. "Baby, you're gonna pay for that." Dallas scooped up a protesting Tasha and carried her into a nearby bedroom.

Tasha's screams echoed through the house. A minute later Dallas emerged, carrying Tasha's bag dress like a trophy. We couldn't stop laughing and Tasha couldn't stop swearing. "Dallas! Bring me back my damn dress!"

Dallas leaned against the living room wall and called down the hallway, "Not until you apologize, dear."

"Dallas, I mean it, goddamn it! You bring that back to me or I'll bite your dick off!"

"If you want your dress so badly, come out here and get it. Frankly, I think you should burn this rag. It looks like a potato sack." He held up the dress for our inspection. It was indeed brown burlap and could have held fifty pounds of potatoes.

Dallas was so engrossed in his fashion show that he didn't see Tasha sneak up behind him, buck naked and wielding a tennis racquet. Her overhead smash lacked form but it conveyed the message. Dallas dropped the dress and ran from the room, screaming and holding his head. Filled with rage, Tasha forgot the dress and chased Dallas into the backyard. We gathered at the bay window, watching the action from a safe distance.

Tasha swung furiously at Dallas who kept screaming, "Not the face! Don't hit me in the face! I'll lose my job!" As a sideline, Dallas performed in a male review and there wasn't much call for battered and bruised strippers.

She taunted him, swinging the racquet back and forth. "You know, Dallas, I used to take lessons. Let's see how much I remember." Her two-handed backhand caught Dallas's rear end. "Apologize, asshole!"

"I'm sorry, Tasha, really." Dallas folded his hands together. He was begging, praying or both.

"Not sincere enough." Her powerful forehand was slow, giving Dallas enough time to back away before Tasha crushed his ribs. Her next forehand connected, and Dallas grabbed his left arm, falling to his knees. Tasha was going for the match.

"Tasha, don't!" Artie commanded. He marched across the lawn, took the racquet and handed Tasha her clothes.

She dressed while the three of them whispered and talked. Tasha slapped Dallas, who retaliated with a "Fuck you!"

Artie calmed them, and they huddled closer. We all watched the mediation from the window. They'd talk, then Tasha would scream or Dallas would scream. Finally Dallas hugged Tasha.

They came inside and we resumed our circle in the living room, Dallas and Tasha locked in an embrace for the rest of the evening. I didn't think it could get any livelier until Debbie the Dictator called my name.

"Kate, Truth or Dare."

There was no way I was telling Debbie any of my secrets. "Dare," I said nervously. For some reason, Debbie hated me. As the stage manager, Debbie had been my boss during the show and she had treated me horribly. I figured she liked Artie and was envious of the attention he gave to me but she'd never said anything to confirm my suspicions. Her eyes narrowed and the corners of her mouth turned up in a devious smile.

"French Kyle," she said casually.

"All right, baby!" Kyle somersaulted into the center of the circle and thrust his pelvis into the air several times.

I started to get up but Artie gripped my arm. "Don't do this," he whispered.

I squeezed his hand. "It's no big deal. It's just a kiss." I stood over Kyle and kicked him in the ass. "Get up Kyle," I said, trying to be cool and hiding my nervousness.

Kyle grabbed my arm and pulled me to the floor. He rolled on top of me, sticking his disgusting tongue deep in my mouth and grinding his hips against me. Everyone was cheering and laughing. His hands squeezed my ass. I'd had enough. I couldn't knee him in the groin so I pushed against his hairy arms. Seeing my resistance, everyone cheered louder, calling Kyle's name and feeding his ego. His belly pressed against me harder, expelling whatever breath was left in my diaphragm. I began to panic. I couldn't breathe and I thought Kyle would crush my ribs. Suddenly Kyle flew off of me and I watched Artie hurl him against the living room wall. He punched Kyle six or seven times before Dallas and Steve McWhirter could pull him away. Kyle dropped to the floor. Both of his eyes were swollen shut and blood flowed from his twisted nose. He couldn't even cry. All he could do was whimper.

Artie tried to free himself from Steve and Dallas, screaming in a mixture of English and Spanish. "I warned you, you fuckin' asshole! Never, never, touch Kate! Next time I'll kill you!"

Artie's rage scared everyone causing the circle to expand. People retreated to the nearest wall, staying away from Artie. I stepped between Artie and Kyle, whispering in Artie's ear and caressing his face. His fists unclenched and his body relaxed. I hugged him and Steve and Dallas backed off.

"Let's go," I said, leading him out the door into an early monsoon. The rain felt fabulous. Artie unlocked the Nova's door but didn't open it. We stood there, allowing the rain to drench us, enjoying the moment. Artie's hands were loosely around my waist and his gray eyes stared into mine.

I didn't know what to do. I was grateful to Artie for saving me from Kyle and I knew what he wanted in return. Succumbing to a lifetime of Catholic guilt, I leaned forward and let him kiss me. His lips were warm and his mustache tickled.

I giggled and he smiled. "What?"

"Um, your mustache."

"I'll shave it off for you tomorrow," he said, pulling me against him for another kiss.

He drove me home and we made out in the Nova for a long time. His hands roamed over my shoulders and my belly, coming dangerously close to my breasts, while his tongue found its way into my mouth. Eventually he lowered me down on my back and extended his body against mine, his erection rubbing against my crotch.

"Jesus, Kate, I want you," he moaned. His lips wandered down into my cleavage, and only then did I realize that smooth Artie had unbuttoned most of my shirt. "Your body is so beautiful." He kissed the slopes of my breasts and his hands started to search for the clasp of my brassiere.

I was dazed. Everything was happening so fast and I was amazed at my own response. Artie's touch felt good and the more he rubbed against me, the more aroused I became. How could this be happening? I needed more time to think.

I tried to sit up. "Artie, I'm not ready for this," I blurted.

He looked up, his eyes filled with lust. "Oh," he said, and it suddenly dawned on him. "You're a virgin, aren't you?"

I nodded. "I mean, it feels good but I don't want to go any further right now."

He caressed my cheek. "I understand. You need some more time. That's okay," he said sweetly.

I buttoned my shirt and Artie walked me to the front door. Before he left, he kissed me deeply, his hands settling into the back pockets of my jeans. His embrace was fierce and possessive and at that moment, he claimed my body and me for his girlfriend.

February 1, 1980

Sis,

You must forgive me if my letter appears to be a bit off. I am presently suffering from a terminal case of sneezecoughflu and have been liberally mixing my scotch with Formula 44 Syrup. It's one hell of a cocktail. My body is once again betraying me, and after all I've done for it!

In your last letter, you mentioned GUILT, and what you had done to make you feel guilty. I'll take them in order: our mother makes you feel guilty. She's an old, Catholic Irishwoman, so it's in the contract. Get used to it. As for your guilt regarding precious Kate and your recent reconnaissance into her bedroom, well, since I'm only an absentee parent at best, I will not judge. I do think you're damn lucky you didn't get caught! I am, however, glad to know that you did not find anything scandalous such as a ten-cent bag, condoms or a bottle of Jack, but that does ruin my Christmas present ideas for her (shucks!). I am a little surprised to hear of a boyfriend. I was beginning to think Kate might be playing for a different team. Oops, I don't want to give you the vapors!

Anyway, back to GUILT. You must realize, dear sister, that when you attack GUILT, you are also attacking the very glue by which our society is held together. Without the benefits of the great god GUILT, fathers would not come home at night and mothers would not keep a clean house. We would all have what the pagans call "one hell of a good time." By paying homage to the great god GUILT, we have been rewarded with such things as the Salk vaccine and hairpins.

Do you know that one bottle of Formula 44 is not like another bottle of Formula 44? Maybe there is a vintage year.

No matter how jaundiced our view of GUILT may be, we are two steps above the crowd that comes in every Saturday to tape the Bible Revival Hour. Reverend Cletus Stampley and his singing family bring Christ into your heart (pronounced 'hort') every Sunday afternoon on KJTP. His wife has a withered left leg, which he constantly kicks when he wants her to hit "E" above high "C." Their daughter also sings. She is a voluptuous teenager, who, if she gets any healthier, will need bodyguards. Reverend Stampley belongs to the old school of Bible thumping. He has been screaming the same sermon for decades—Jesus Will Get You if You Don't Watch Out.

What is it with such people? I don't blame my friends for turning from the church. People like Stampley have reduced the figure of Jesus to that of a cosmic Al Capone offering protection to a bunch of cowering merchants. Maybe Jesus carried a knife. I know Simon Peter did. He cut off some guy's ear at Gethsemane.

My point is that I am tired of people who threaten others, and I am tired of people who spend most of their emotional currency in getting others to feel guilty. And, in my opinion, religionists do more than anyone else. When you attack guilt, you are attacking the very foundations of the Holy Mother Church.

I might go back to church if they started dipping the wafers in Formula 44.

On a clerical note—H&R Block lost my W-2 forms. Hee hee. I don't think I'll file this year anyway. I'm going to owe them a lot. Nestor and I have a scheme. We are going to list one another as legal guardian and send in testimonies that each of us is dead. Might work. If not then you will begin to receive a series of letters we can call "The Prison Years."

I think I'll kill this last bottle of Formula 44 and lay my beleaguered head down for a while.

A litany of love for you all,
Charles

The Awakening

"I have an announcement," my mother said one evening at dinner. My father and I looked up at her while my brother and sister continued to make forts out of their mashed potatoes.

"I've been approached by several people to run for the school board." She beamed from ear to ear.

"That's great!" my father exclaimed. He leaned over and kissed my mother, causing my siblings to wail in disgust. "You're the best choice. I'm so proud of you!"

"What does the school board really do?" I asked with my typical sixteen-year-old cynicism.

"Kate, the school board oversees all of the schools and the superintendent. The board makes the decisions that affect all of the students in the district."

I started to smile. "Does that mean you'd be Principal Counts' boss?" I'd never forgiven my old principal for forbidding the girls from dancing together.

My mother laughed. "Well, not directly, honey. The governing board oversees the superintendent and Principal Counts works for him."

"Oh," I said, nodding. Mom just needed to have a little talk with the superintendent. "So, when do you start?"

My mother shook her head while she cut her pork chop. "I have to be elected, Kate, in the election in November. Enough people will need to vote for me and if I win, then I get to be on the board." She looked at me and smiled. "I'd like the whole family to help me with the campaign."

"Sure," I said, hoping that this campaign didn't interfere with softball, which was coming up in a few weeks.

"Are you going out with Artie tonight?" my father asked.

"Of course she is!" my mother gushed. "It's Friday night. Are you two going to the movies?"

Without looking up, I said, "Uh, actually I'm going over to Beth's tonight. Artie and I broke up."

"Why?" she asked. "Are the two of you fighting?"

I shook my head and shrugged my shoulders. "It just isn't going to work out."

"You want to be friends only," my father concluded. "Right?"

I glanced at him and nodded, grateful for his support.

"I don't believe this!" my mother interrupted. "Kate, you and Artie have been going together for a while. Don't you think you should give Artie a chance?"

I steeled myself for her arguments. I couldn't figure out why Artie was so important to her but she was clearly his advocate. "Mom, I have given it a chance. I just don't feel that way about him."

"Then why would it take you so long to realize it?" Her voice became shrill as her emotions got to her. "If that's the case, then it seems you were stringing him along."

I shrugged my shoulders and shook my head. "I wasn't trying to be cruel to him. It's not like I haven't tried."

"Well, maybe you should try harder," she said. Her voice was filled with Catholic judgment and my anger surfaced.

"If you must know, we broke up because I wouldn't sleep with him."

The room went silent and my mother's mouth fell open. I watched my father's face turn beet red and he glared at my mother.

"Let me get this straight," he whispered, in a voice that was soft and deadly. "Artie was pressuring you to have sex?"

"No, Dad. Artie didn't pressure me to do anything. Before you ask, yes, there was some touching and lots of kissing but my virginity is still intact. And now, I really don't want to talk about this anymore." I stood and picked up my plate. "Now, if I may be excused, I'm going to Beth's house."

They nodded, too shocked at the truth. As I drove to Beth's, I imagined they would spend the evening debating my bombshell. My father didn't like Artie, not because Artie was a horrible person, but he suspected what my mother did not—I had no real feelings for Artie except as a friend.

After I had told Artie I wasn't ready for sex, our relationship rewound backward and it took Artie almost a month to kiss me again. Two months later he made it to second base, his hands groping my breasts as we kissed good night. I began to think he was literally marking days on a calendar because two months after the first grope, during a make out session in his room, he unbuttoned my shirt and whispered in my ear, "I want to touch you."

"Okay," I said nervously, still not entirely sure I wanted to go any further but feeling that there were only two choices, stop completely or move forward. The decision was made in a moment and my shirt and bra were quickly discarded.

We had remained firmly planted somewhere between second and third base for the last month. Whatever initial interest I had experienced when Artie first touched me had evaporated by the third time we'd made out. Now his touch was a chore and if I wanted to experience any feeling, I conjured images of women, particularly Beth.

Artie had made numerous attempts to unbutton my jeans and touch my nether regions, only to be met by a mental wall in my mind and the very real feeling of my hand pushing him away. I could not go any further. Every time he would tug at my zipper, I would gently return his wandering hand to my breast and whisper, "Here."

Allowing Artie to totally undress me set off a chain reaction of scenarios in my mind that ended with his penis inside me—something

I couldn't fathom. There was safety in remaining half dressed but each time he was thwarted, I knew his frustration level rose and his reaction to the rejection sharpened, until finally one afternoon he couldn't take it anymore.

As I pushed his hand away, he sat up in disgust. "Jesus, Kate, why won't you let me touch you?"

"Artie, I'm just not ready."

He groaned and threw his hands up in the air. "We've been stuck in this place for a month! Don't get me wrong, I love sucking on your breasts and kissing your mouth, but I love you, and I want to *make* love to you." He spoke softly and pushed me down on the bed. His body slid on top of mine, while he caressed my face with kisses and his hands fondled my breasts. "I love you," he whispered, over and over.

His tongue invaded my mouth and he lifted himself high enough for his fingers to reach into the waistband of my jeans. My body stiffened as he stroked my lower abdomen and brushed against my pubic hair. "Relax," he cooed. "Just let me see you. I promise we won't have sex. I just want to see your beautiful body. Please, Kate."

He looked into my eyes, begging. Unaccustomed to wielding power, especially over a man, I nodded. He smiled and gently pulled down my zipper, peeling my jeans away. My heart raced as I realized that only my thin, nylon panties stood between me and nakedness.

His hands stroked my thighs and his breathing was ragged. "This feels so right."

Hmm. Not the best choice of words.

Alarm bells sounded in my mind. Suddenly the male picture from *Gray's Anatomy* appeared in front of me, all of the arrows now pointing at Artie's parts, one in particular that was bulging through his jeans.

Just as his fingers reached for my panties, I grabbed his hands, shaking my head furiously. "Artie, I can't. I just can't."

His look of defeat almost made me change my mind but I closed my mouth to prevent the words from forming. He crawled off of me and lay down on the other side of the bed, facing away.

"I'm sorry," I said, quickly re-dressing. "I can't explain my feelings. It's not you. You're not doing anything wrong."

"I'm obviously not doing anything right either."

I couldn't think of what to say. I had no worldly experience to guide me. Artie was the first person who had ever kissed me or touched me and yet, I felt nothing, certainly not the interest or excitement that he felt. I debated for a split second about uttering the truth to him, telling him that every nerve in my body tingled when Beth smiled at me but the idea left almost as quickly as it came. Arturo Ortega, machismo Hispanic male, would come unglued if he knew that what he had in common with his girlfriend was an interest in women.

I stood there, dressed, waiting for him to turn over, hoping he would say something. When he didn't, I just left, without grace or closure but at least with my virginity and part of my dignity.

I recounted everything to Beth up in her tree house. When I started to cry, she pulled me close, the scent of the perfume I'd given her for Christmas comforting me. I closed my eyes, enjoying the curves of her body, the softness of her skin, and the beat of her heart.

"I'm glad you broke up," she said. "He wasn't right for you."

"I know. It's not that he wasn't nice to me. He was. Why couldn't I like him? Maybe there's something wrong with me," I added.

"There's nothing wrong with you," she said. Her fingers stroked my hair and I involuntarily sighed in pleasure.

"Do you like it when I touch you?" she asked quietly. I realized Beth's heartbeat had quickened and it was pounding in my ear.

I gazed up at her. The moonlight shone through the window, illuminating Beth's beautiful face in its glow. She was an angel.

When I didn't answer, she caressed my cheek with her hand. "Kate."

I couldn't breathe. Her saying my name caused more physical reaction in my body than Artie's months of groping and kissing. I was still a relationship novice and I had no idea what to do—again. The elevator inside me was plunging. I stared at the pupils of her green eyes until they closed and her lips pressed against mine. I sat there, realizing a woman was kissing me. This wasn't a grandma kiss or the innocent kiss of a friend, but a passionate, tender, sensual kiss.

She ran her hands down my back and my mind went away. It floated out of the tree house and my senses took over. They showed me the tantalizing realities of her round, soft body, musky perfume mixed with her intimate smell, the quick, high-pitched gasps that escaped from her lips as each kiss flowed into another and the sweet, wonderful taste of her mouth. Only our curiosity at discovering each other's reactions forced us to part.

"God, what was that?" I panted.

"C'mon, Kate," she laughed. "We've been making passes at each other since eighth grade! I can't believe you don't know how I feel about you."

I couldn't believe that all this time she'd wanted me as much as I'd wanted her. "Beth, I just never thought . . . Beth, are you a lesbian?"

She smiled at the word. "Uh-huh. And so are you," she said as her left hand unbuttoned my shirt.

"Beth, I don't know what I am. Maybe I'm a lesbian."

She laughed and her hand traced the outline of my collarbone. "Oh, no? Then what was that kiss?"

"Well, to some extent," I said analytically, "that was curiosity."

"Well, then you were pretty damn curious," she cracked. "Your tongue was so far down my throat I thought I was going to swallow it."

"Are you really a lesbian?"

She nodded.

"When did you know?"

"I've known for a long time. I didn't do anything about it until we got to high school, until someone propositioned me."

"Who?" I asked quickly.

"Tasha."

My mouth dropped open. "Tasha? Tasha was gay?"

"Tasha was bi," Beth corrected.

"How? When?" The questions and answers were coming too quickly. My brain was overloading.

"Do you remember the party where Artie fought with Kyle?"

How could I forget?

"Well, Tasha asked me to stay after everyone else left."

"Uh-huh."

"She told me she was attracted to me and we started kissing."

The conflict inside me was paralyzing. I just sat there, watching her fingers unhook the front of my bra and gently part the polyester fabric. Her hands cupped my breasts and her thumbs fondled my hardening nipples, betraying any denial I might have spoken.

"I can't believe you never figured it out, Kate."

"I just didn't think . . ." My voice trailed off. My mind could only focus on the pleasure of Beth's touch. "How many lovers have you had?"

"Only Tasha and one other person, someone you don't know."

"Who?" I asked anyway.

"It's not important, Kate. What is important is that I love you. I've always loved you."

"Why are you telling me now?" I spoke in a whisper, my mouth full of dust. This was a stark comparison to the wetness that was growing between my thighs with every movement of Beth's hand.

"Because it feels right. I want to be your first."

"You want us to be lovers?"

"No Kate, I want us to be drag queens. Of course I want to be your lover, stupid!" Her face disappeared between my breasts.

"Beth, stop. We need to figure this out." Before I could protest further, her tongue found my nipple and created a chain reaction through my body. Every nerve tingled and I thought I was having a heart attack.

I watched her mouth drift to my stomach until she arrived at the zipper of my shorts.

I could see one eye through the tussle of hair that covered my abdomen. "Kate, I'm only going to ask once. Do you want me to stop?"

"No."

December 11, 1980

Dear Sis,

I tried to call you on your birthday, but I got no answer. So, allow me now to wish you a very happy birthday. I hope you live another forty-five years. Myself, I'll be dead by Thursday.

Congratulations on your recent election victory. I know you have always told me you would like to sit in the state legislature, and this is clearly a first step toward that goal. Just try to remember the little people.

Yesterday was my day off and I thought it would be nice to take our resident puppy for some exercise at the park. Our puppy dog is the creature who suffers from terminal paranoia. She stays in the basement all day long and will lapse into an immediate coma if you notice her existence.

Right across the street from the park is a tavern, so I thought I would take the puppy dog and tie her to a tree (which is like tethering a rock to a rock) and get myself a beer. It didn't quite work out that way. As soon as the sunlight hit the puppy dog, she began to whine and show signs of having a seizure, so

I did the next best thing. I put her in a brown grocery bag and carried her thusly to the park. She seemed to like the ride. Once we got the park, she again refused to come out of the grocery bag, so I attached the leash to a tree and tied the other end around the grocery bag. Then I went for a beer. Upon my return, I found a pretty four-year-old girl staring at the grocery bag.

"What is that?" she said, pointing.

"That's my pet grocery bag," I responded.

"What's its name?"

"Master Weyerhauser."

"Can I pet it?"

"Sure."

"Grocery bags don't bite, do they?"

"Not as a rule."

She stroked the bag, gave me a big smile, and went running off down the road, shouting to her mother that she wanted a pet grocery bag. The child will, no doubt, be in therapy before the week is out.

Regarding my employment, the big news is—I still am. Of course, this is after a few "incidences." In fact, I'm now meeting celebrities.

I met Congressman Morris Udall this week. He was in the studio for an interview. Our newscaster introduced us. Udall said, "How do you do? Don't screw it up." I laughed and set up his microphone.

As we were preparing for the interview, I turned on the intercom from the booth and said, "Mr. Udall, the first question of the evening will be, Is it true that you were thrown out of the American Nazi Party on a morals charge?"

The poor guy couldn't stop laughing. We almost had to call off the interview. During the breaks I kept quoting from "Ozymandias" which didn't help. It's not every day you get to see a grown Congressman cry.

The next week I was fired because I kept bringing a bottle of scotch to work with me. Harry, my boss, wouldn't stand for it. (He quit smoking last month, so now he thinks anyone can quit anything—idiot.) Right after he fired me he rehired me because he can't find another director who'll work for the federal minimum wage. We compromised. I promised not to drink on the job but I have permission to come to work completely SWACKED.

As for your concerns regarding the fair Kate, remember, she is deep within the teen years. If it feels as though she's shutting you out, she probably is. But this is only temporary until the frontal lobes of the brain and its chemistry catch up to the temporal lobe, well . . . whatever. Encourage her to visit me, and I'll psychoanalyze her fragile teen psyche. I'm sure I can get to the bottom of her troubles. What would probably work better is if I get her totally stoned and drunk. Then I'm sure she will tell all. Do I have your permission?

On another note, one which I hate to even mention, I have recently undergone a little procedure called a proctostomy, which is another term for "rectal hell." I had noticed that my body had been bleeding from places that were inappropriate. Not to say that a man bleeding on any regular basis is normal, because this is, of course, how we know God is a MAN. We men are way too squeamish to face a "monthly bill" or pregnancy.

You see, until now, I've prescribed to the "ostrich approach" to life. If you don't see it, it can't possibly be all that bad. I went and met the deceptive Dr. Quornos. I call her deceptive because initially she came across as a caring, humane person. Given the nature of my malady I was prepared to undergo a certain amount of undignified examination, but I had no idea that I was to be violated by an instrument, which judging from its effect, was slightly smaller than your garden variety telephone pole. What is more, the good Dr. Quornos enjoyed it. She probably reads a lot of Betty Friedan.

While the good doctor was trailblazing across my already overly taxed body, it occurred to me that Anita Bryant might have been right all along. You have got to have a rather sick mind to enjoy any anal activity, beyond taking a really good dump. I kept screaming, "I'm a Catholic! I'll have to go to confession!" It didn't work. She just giggled and kept probing away.

Afterward she gave me a box of suppositories and told me to use one a day. Fat chance. The things are the size of dill pickles. Well, it is now time for me to perform my morning ablutions and prepare to go to work. I have a little ritual I go through each morning. I rise and brush my hair. I pour a drink. I spit at my suppositories and then become supremely indifferent to the CBS Morning News.

At any rate, do not worry yourself about my health. My body and I have a deal, and I'm sure it will keep its end of the bargain. You just worry about the Wright Elementary School District. Go get 'em!

Your so very proud and always healthy brother,
Charles

Present Day

What do you get the woman who needs nothing, wants nothing and can use nothing for her birthday? She cannot cultivate a new interest like stamp collecting, learn a new skill such as knitting and worst of all, she cannot participate in the pastimes that brought her the greatest joy before. Her life has been reduced to a fifteen-by-fifteen-foot room with a small closet and a hospital bed. She has a nightstand that holds her glass of water and a picture of our family but there is little space for anything else. Her closet is full of clothes she will hardly wear and the one wall that is her own is already covered with photographs and memories. What few personal things she brought, such as movies for her TV/video unit, have already wandered away to other rooms, never to be seen again.

We've only been in Target for forty-five minutes and my patience has withered to zero, exhausted during our hunt for an appropriate card, which is surprisingly traumatic for me. All of the messages seem insensitive, stating words of hope or vitality.

"Each birthday brings you the gift of a year that has never been lived before," I read out loud. I set that one aside for a yellow card with a dog sitting inside a convertible. "Who knows where this year will take you? Enjoy the ride!" I sigh, the arguments for quality of life screaming in my brain.

"What about one with a sincere message?" Sarah suggests. She shows me a beautiful lace card with several stanzas of flowing italicized script.

I shake my head. "I'll have to read her the whole thing."

"Is that a problem?"

"I'd like to get something with a few words and very large print. Maybe she'll remember it."

Sarah returns the sentimental card and we resume our search, which consumes the better part of a half hour. We finally settle on a cute Snoopy card and I am in a foul mood. We've resorted to cartoon characters usually reserved for a five-year-old.

Sarah and I wander up and down the aisles searching for a gift, something that will be meaningful to my mother and practical for her life. We hope that the perfect idea will spring from the shelves, something we have not already contemplated or rejected.

"You could get her a car polisher," Sarah says with a grin. I chuckle at her humor.

"No," I answer. "I'd get her the thigh flexer before I'd buy the car polisher."

Sarah puts her arm around me and kisses me on the cheek. "We'll find something, don't worry. The store might be closed by the time we do but your mother *will* have a gift."

She has a determined look on her face, one that is always comforting to me. She is my safe harbor, my confessor and, at times, my second mother.

"Have I told you today that I love you?"

She smiles and pushes the cart toward women's socks, an aisle that actually looks more promising than car care. There are plenty of slippers, which might be a good choice.

Two hours later we enter the checkout line with a Snoopy card, some slippers and a video poker game, which she may or may not be able to use. I quickly dial up my siblings while we wait in line.

"What are you doing?" Sarah asks.

"I'm calling Tommy and Karen and placing dibs on these gifts. Let them come up with their own ideas."

Sarah rolls her eyes. While I'm on the phone leaving messages, she holds up one of those tabloids and points at the cover photo, a rather unflattering picture of my first lover, Beth.

I shake my head in disbelief, seriously doubting that she has given birth to an alien love child. Sarah flips through the pages, finding the article. She scans the paragraphs, laughing heartily.

"So did Beth's alien baby have one or two heads?" I slip the phone back in my purse and lean over her shoulder. The main photo is of Beth and her lover, Kristin, at a gala premier. Next to them is a large purple alien in the background.

"I think it's a plug for her new movie," Sarah concludes.

"Either that or we've become aunts."

The Fortune Teller

"Twenty miles to Tucson," Beth announced as we whizzed by a highway sign. "How far is it from the city limits?"

"Only about ten minutes," I said, chomping on a french fry.

"It'll be cool seeing your uncle again even though it's only for a few days."

I nodded my agreement but didn't say anything.

We glanced at each other simultaneously. "You know, Kate, I'm really glad we're taking this trip. I think you need it."

"I do."

"Are you okay?" she asked, massaging the back of my neck.

"Yeah," I said, flashing a nearly-sincere smile and trying to give her some reassurance as to my emotional state, although I wasn't sure how I felt.

She rested her chin on my shoulder. "Do you think your uncle will suspect?"

"I hope not."

"Don't you think we should tell him?"

"Beth, are you crazy? My uncle and my mother are very close. I could just see it. 'Barbara, I loved visiting with your daughter, the lesbian!'"

She laughed at my impression but it died away quickly. "I just figured he'd be the one adult who'd understand."

She was right. He would understand but I wasn't sure about my mother. The past three months had been a never ending roller coaster ride for my emotions. Since Beth and I had become lovers, I found my passion and happiness soaring to heights I never imagined were possible. At the same time, my Catholic guilt was at Vatican proportions since I spent quite a bit of time lying to my parents. Sister Mary wouldn't have been pleased.

Of course, they were really only half lies since I said I was going out with Beth, which was the truth. But I knew they assumed *going out* meant going to the movies or the mall, not up to Beth's tree house to make love. I'd always spent a lot of time with Beth and been overly affectionate toward her in their presence. They were used to seeing us this way but they'd always dismissed it as typical female bonding. At least that part was the truth. Beth and I were certainly bonding.

"Kate, are you paying attention to the road?"

I blinked and pulled the car back to our side of the white highway stripe, very aware that Beth was rubbing my thigh. Her hand wandered up my leg and I laughed. "And do you really think you're helping?" I responded.

She snuggled against me. "I love you. I'll always love you."

"I love you," I said, wrapping my free arm around her.

The industrial outskirts of the city soon vanished and the familiar signs of a college town appeared—apartment complexes, bars and thrift stores. We drove through the University of Arizona and Beth pointed out the various sights, such as her future dorm and the theatre department where she would spend most of her time.

U of A was a done deal for Beth. Her entire family had attended the "U," most recently her two older sisters. Beth had entertained momentary thoughts of applying to UCLA's film school but the family brainwashing proved stronger, especially since her father refused to finance her education anywhere else. All she could do now was imagine life as a Wildcat.

We headed into an old residential area. All of the houses were adobe but each had its own personality and sharply contrasted from its neighbors. Styles varied greatly from the richly ornate to the overtly tacky, a Pepto Bismol monstrosity situated next to a photo spread opportunity for *Architectural Digest*; a meticulously manicured lawn crouched between two candidates for repossession. Truly eclectic, truly Tucson.

Uncle Charlie's place was easy to find—the only house on the block with a room above the garage, his room. Beth and I trudged up the wooden stairs, classical music permeating the walls. We knocked several times until he finally opened the door.

"Kate!" He lifted me off the ground and we pirouetted into the room.

Uncle Charlie's small apartment was only a few hundred square feet. Although most wouldn't suspect, my uncle's scraggly appearance did not mirror his living habits. Shelves lined two walls, filled with nothing but hardbound books on almost every subject imaginable and alphabetized by author. The only other extravagance was his stereo, a system which included much more than just a turntable and tape deck, I'd dubbed it the Enterprise since I couldn't even figure out how to turn the damn thing on. His living room furniture consisted of a sofa sleeper and coffee table. Noticeably missing was a TV, an ironic statement from a man who'd worked in television most of his adult life.

We spent the afternoon exchanging family gossip. Beth, having met almost the entire Mitchell and Driscoll clans, loved hearing our stories. She claimed her family was dull and dry. We were Technicolor, they were black and white.

By sundown my uncle was drunk. He'd polished off a bottle of J.D. and was opening a six-pack.

"Want one?" he said to me and Beth.

"Sure," we responded.

"Hah. You can't have one. Everybody knows the legal drinking age in this apartment is sixteen."

"We're sixteen," Beth commented. I nodded.

"Quick, when were your birthdays?"

Beth and I recited our birthdays simultaneously. Uncle Charlie threw us each a beer and brought out a tray of hoagies. We ate while he told stories until Beth had to beg him to stop for fear of tossing up her dinner.

"Charlie, do you really know people who live in the sewers?" Beth asked cynically.

"Several."

"You're full of it," Beth said playfully.

"Well, then I guess I'll have to prove it to you lovely young ladies. Tomorrow we go underground." He raised his beer for a toast and we clinked cans.

"How about Monopoly?" I asked. Beth voiced her agreement and I went in search of my uncle's only board game.

Next to my grandmother, I loved playing Monopoly with my uncle. We'd never finished a game in our entire lives. For some reason, moving our pieces around the board and purchasing the properties led to philosophical discussions that soon overrode any desire we had to win.

He rolled the dice and dropped his cannon onto Marvin Gardens. "Did I ever tell you I knew a Marvin and he owned a garden?"

We both shook our heads.

"Was it some kind of a nursery?" Beth asked.

"Nursery's a good word but he only grew one plant."

"What'd he grow?" I asked, picking up the dice.

"Cannabis."

"You mean pot?" Beth said.

"Exactly." His expression turned stern. "Has either of you ladies puffed the weed?"

We both shook our heads and Uncle Charlie nodded his approval. "Good. Should you ever decide you would like to experiment, please contact me. I'll make sure you're purchasing uncontaminated, quality goods." I shook the dice, ready to roll but Uncle Charlie held up a hand. "Kate, before we continue and while I'm still coherent enough to hear this story, I want to know how long you two have been lovers."

The dice dropped to the board, sending houses everywhere. My uncle popped two more beers and handed one to each of us. "Here, you both look like you could use this."

"How did you guess?" Beth asked. We knew there was no point in hiding it from him now. He was too smart and we respected him too much to lie to him after he'd stated the truth.

Uncle Charlie laughed. "Guess? I didn't have to guess." He motioned toward the two of us sprawled out on his floor, bodies close together, legs intertwined, and Beth's hand resting on top of mine. The beer and my uncle's company had destroyed our inhibitions. It was amazing we still had our clothes on.

I said the first thing that came to my mind. "Charlie, please don't tell Mom. She doesn't suspect anything and I don't know what she'd do if she knew."

"Kate's right," Beth added. "Telling you is one thing but our folks are another. I mean, you're cool and well . . ." Beth searched for her words in her beer can. "Well, they're our parents."

Uncle Charlie chuckled. "I appreciate the compliment." He paused and thumbed through his stack of Monopoly money. "First of all, I'm not going to tell anyone anything but I also think you're not giving your parents enough credit." He looked at Beth momentarily but let his gaze settle on me. "Especially you, Kate. I know your mother seems like some conservative Reaganite but she really has a liberal heart. Think about it."

He got up and headed for his closet-like bedroom, too drunk to remember we hadn't played the game. Before he closed the door, he turned and looked at Beth and me. "By the way, I think you make a cute couple."

The next day Uncle Charlie kept his promise. By ten o'clock we were cruising to the edge of Tucson in search of sewer people. He turned onto a dirt road and the van became the center of a dust storm. We drove for several miles, veering south until we came to an exposed concrete pipe. It rose out of the ground like the mouth of a giant monster. A wrought iron gate, cut to fit the circular opening, swung freely in the wind. A metal sign affixed to the frame reminded workers to KEEP GATE LOCKED AT ALL TIMES.

My uncle led us into the pipe, which eventually dead-ended at a wall of dirt.

"Down we go," he said, pointing to a ladder on the ground. We looked into the blackness beyond the first two rungs. Beth and I exchanged worried glances but followed Uncle Charlie into the abyss.

"Flashlights on," he commanded. Three small streams of light danced around the concrete walls. We were in a long pipe that stretched far beyond the capabilities of our flashlights. We walked single file, Uncle Charlie singing "Alice's Restaurant" along the way. The pipe was filthy but dry, only a small trail of wet residue lining the bottom. This area hadn't seen sewage for a long time.

We turned several corners and I felt the ground sloping downward. My uncle had just finished the fifth verse of the Arlo Guthrie standard when we arrived at our destination, some sort of anteroom extending from the end of a pipe. I didn't know how it got there and I didn't care. This whole thing was too much like a Stephen King novel for my tastes.

The niche was the size of a closet, an old Army cot hugged one wall, a makeshift kitchen against the opposite wall. Between them sat an old woman on an orange crate and in front of her was a steamer trunk covered with bottles of colored liquid and vials of herbs. A Coleman lantern illuminated her face and the object she held, a large round rock.

She had the face of a dried apple and a long, vulture-like nose. She smiled, revealing nothing but gums. Her T-shirt proclaimed, "Hell Raiser," (a sympathy I found strikingly accurate) and hung over a pair of loose fitting old-lady jeans.

A shriek stopped my heart. Beth and I clung to each other.

"Look," said my uncle, pointing to a high corner. Above the bed on a perch sat a large green parrot.

"Frito. Frito. Frito," he squawked.

"Why is he saying Frito?" I asked Uncle Charlie.

"That's his name. And this, ladies, is Consuela Consuela." He pointed to the old woman, who nodded. "Consuela Consuela, my niece and her friend don't believe you live down here."

"Of course I do. How else can I escape the rotten government and its evil taxes?" Her thick Spanish accent reminded me of Artie's grandmother. "Just now, I'm putting a curse on President Reagan." She held up the rock and recited an incantation, her soft mumbling increasing in volume and emotion. Soon Frito was squawking away and their voices echoed throughout the tunnels. Soliloquy complete, she set the rock on the trunk and kissed it.

"What's so great about that rock?" Beth asked.

Consuela Consuela laughed. "Foolish girl, this isn't a rock. It's a hairball, from a big steer."

"Oh, gross," Beth whined. My face conveyed equal displeasure.

"Not gross," Consuela Consuela corrected. "This hairball has powers and is magical. I see things through it."

"Could you tell us our fortunes?" Beth asked excitedly.

"Oh yes," Consuela Consuela replied.

Suddenly Frito swooped down and landed on Consuela Consuela's shoulder. "Frito!" he cried.

Consuela Consuela looked at the bird. "All right, but only one. Too many Fritos for Frito and I have to take a bath." Her hand reached down behind the trunk and reappeared with a Frito in her hand. The chip disappeared in a millisecond.

"Now, what were we talking about?" She looked at each of us.

"You were going to predict their futures," my uncle reminded.

"Of course. Which of you goes first?"

"I will," Beth volunteered.

"Good. Now bring that other crate over here and sit next to me. I must touch you."

Beth grabbed a crate and sat next to the lantern. I couldn't help noticing how the light accentuated her beauty.

Consuela Consuela took Beth's hand and began chanting. Frito paced across the old woman's shoulders, squawking the entire time. When the chanting faded away, Consuela Consuela took a deep breath and giggled.

"You have a very exciting life in front of you, my dear. I see fame, fortune and deep love. Tell me young lady, are you in the performing arts?"

"Yes," Beth cried. "Am I going to be famous?"

"Most definitely. You will experience great love with a naked yellow man."

"What?" I blurted.

"I'm going to fall in love with a naked yellow man?" Beth spoke slowly, making sure she had the prophecy correct.

"That's what I see," Consuela Consuela said proudly.

Now we were sure she was a crackpot.

Frito pecked at her head. "All right, all right, Frito. One more." Again, the hand went to some mysterious place and withdrew a chip. Snap and it was devoured.

"You are next," Consuela Consuela said to me.

I shook my head, not wanting to know my future.

"Come on, Kate, it's fun," Beth coaxed.

"Yeah, Kate," my uncle added. "I didn't bring you down here for nothing. I want to know when you'll make enough money to support your loving family members, especially your generous and thoughtful uncle."

I reluctantly took Beth's place on the crate and grasped Consuela Consuela's skeletal hand. She chanted. Frito paced and squawked. When she opened her eyes, she stared at me. Hard. I could see my life and my memories being sucked out of me and into her brain over some sort of mental bridge between our heads.

"What's wrong?" Beth asked.

She blinked and her face softened. She squeezed my hand. "Your life will be a true journey, with some great hardships. You will take the first step when Richard Cory dies."

"When?" I asked.

"When Richard Cory dies."

"Who?" Beth asked. She was bewildered. I glanced at my smiling uncle but he pretended to examine his nails when our eyes met. "Somebody named Richard Cory is going to die and make life easier for Kate?" Beth looked at me, but I shrugged my shoulders. I didn't know anyone named Richard Cory or Dick Cory or Ricky Cory.

Consuela Consuela offered to foretell my uncle's future, but he declined. He'd already seen it during an acid trip in '69.

We spent several hours listening to Consuela Consuela tell stories of her childhood in Tijuana. When we finally emerged from the sewers, slightly drunk from some disgusting drink she called "swill," the sun was going down. We were surprised, having lost complete track of time underground. We watched the sunset before piling into the van and finding our way back to civilization.

If I'd had the gift of prophecy, I would have dragged Consuela Consuela out of that sewer and taken her to the track. We could have made millions. Very soon, I would meet Richard Cory, and many years later, Beth would fall in love with a naked yellow man, her Academy Award for Best Actress.

October 3, 1981

Sis,

My emergency surgery here at the VA went quite well. A triple bypass on one's liver does two things—requires one to quit drinking, FOREVER, and creates an internal system similar to the LA freeways.

You expressed to me some interest on how a federal hospital operates and since I have some time on my hands, I thought I would respond. At the moment, my nurse, who graduated from the Earl Scheib School of Practical Nursing and Lawn Mower Repair, is off mixing another glass of "medication." Just what the medication is supposed to do is something of a mystery to me. It tastes like chalk and taco sauce with a pinch of Estee Lauder skin cream.

There are other nurses—Registered Nurses—most of who seem to know what they are doing. Remember one thing: Never ask a nurse how she is doing that day! They will actually drop whatever they are doing and tell you.

The doctors seem to work hard, though much of their time is spent chasing nurses and wondering why they didn't go into a law partnership with their brother.

Keep in mind that everything is painted INDUSTRIAL GREEN. Even the coffee looks green. The meat loaf looks green but it is supposed to. Most medicine is green, except for BARIUM, which is pink. It is pink because it is RADIOACTIVE. I had two pink treatments and I expect to glow in the dark for the rest of my life.

All in all, a federal hospital is like any other. Some may look nicer than others, but they all amount to the same thing—they are all full of sick people who are afraid. So if you ever have a friend who must spend time in a hospital, take time to visit him or her (and don't say anything about how green they look).

Thanks for the article. I always knew you'd make headlines, and fortunately, these don't require an investigation by the attorney general. You will make an excellent school board president. Can I assume there will be a legislative race in your future? Is it only a matter of time before we address you as governor? Just remember, I have big plans.

Give everyone my love. I look forward to seeing you when I'm not green.

Always,
Charlie

The Christmas Extravaganza

"Where are the elves?" I demanded of Alex Underwood, a stagehand. He shrugged his overdeveloped shoulders and waddled away with a six-foot candy cane. I tapped my clipboard, gazing about stage right for the six preschoolers who'd agreed to be elves at the annual Valley High Christmas Pageant. Seeing no one except the untalented dance troupe, I maneuvered through the dancers and around the backstage area.

The annual Christmas pageant was THE event of the year, the union of the entire fine arts department. This was one of two times during the school year that the choir, orchestra, dance troupe and theatre combined their talents, the other time being the spring musical. Practically the entire community attended the pageant, which was much more than just a high school show. Each year was an attempt at surpassing the achievements of the previous pageant and the city gathered to see if that goal was attained. No one thought last year's pageant, which included Santa's helicopter landing on the auditorium roof, could be topped. They didn't know what I knew—this year's pageant was the best.

For me that translated into the worst two weeks of my life. As the technical director, I was assigned the difficult position of stage manager. It was my job to coordinate all three hundred participants, including some animal cast members. To say the least, rehearsals had been interesting. One of the sheep bit a six-year-old elf and the animal had to be quarantined for two days. The donkey had wandered onto the archery field and nearly been skewered. The worst headaches, though, came from the non-theatrically inclined humans who couldn't tell stage right from stage left.

I was going crazy. At this very moment, the choir was finishing what it considered to be a moving rendition of "O Little Town of Bethlehem" and would immediately segue into "Up on the Housetop." Six elves were to dance with them, if I ever found the little rugrats.

Beth approached, dressed as the Virgin Mary. "How's it going?" she whispered.

"It's not," I snapped. "Where are those kids?"

"Calm down," she said, massaging my shoulders.

I closed my eyes. It felt wonderful. "I don't have time for this, Beth," I said opening my eyes.

"Yes, you do." She pointed across the stage to the wings. There were the six elves, lined up and ready to go.

"How did they get past me?"

"They're small. Now come here." She led me to an empty chair, pushed me down and kneaded my arms and shoulders.

"Beth, I've got things to do." I started to get up but she pushed me back into the chair.

"In a minute. You're so tense, Kate."

"I have a reason to be tense. This show is a nightmare waiting to happen. About a hundred things could go wrong and it'll be on my head if anything does."

"It's just a show. Don't worry about it."

"Easy for you to say. All you have to do is sit in front of the cradle and look virginal."

"Quite an acting performance, don't you think?"

Before I could comment, Ryan Winslow, stagehand-in-training

appeared. "Kate, Mr. Mayes is looking for you."

"Great." I removed Beth's wonderful hands and followed him back to a distraught Mr. Mayes.

"Kate, where have you been?" he asked desperately.

"Just over on stage left."

He grabbed my arm firmly. "Kate, stay here. I need you by me. I need to be sure everything is flowing. You are my island in this tempest-tossed sea."

I nodded sympathetically. I liked Mr. Mayes but he wasn't a technical person. He was a melodramatic actor who'd spent too many summers performing Greek tragedies.

The dancers pranced onto the stage for a lively rendition of "Sleigh Ride." They actually weren't that bad, and it would have been their best number, except for Wendy Reed, the ozone queen. As the song ended and the dancers dashed off, Wendy smashed against the steel tension cable that extended from the floor to the catwalks high above the stage. Everyone gasped as Wendy bounced back onto the stage, twirled about and then fell to the floor unconscious.

The choir director ran to the fallen prima donna, while the dancers hovered above their comrade, holding each others' hands and crying. The school nurse appeared and after a quick examination, each dancer grabbed a limb and carried Wendy off.

Mr. Mayes was livid and I really wanted to tell him to go take one of the Valiums he stashed in his desk drawer but I thought better of it. Instead, I spent the next three songs calming him, assuring him that the show was a great success.

We prepared for the final song, "Silent Night." This was to be the crowning touch to a perfect concert. Besides the choir singing the Christmas classic with the orchestra's accompaniment, Mr. Mayes had planned a visual extravaganza as well. We had spent the last two months building a loft above the choir, literally a second story to the stage. While the audience listened to "Silent Night," they could watch the shepherds and kings assemble in the stable to worship the baby Jesus, the only non-living creature in the picture. The donkeys, sheep and even the camel were real. Mr. Mayes envisioned the audience leaving with tears in their eyes after experiencing one of the greatest spectacles ever attempted on a high school stage. It truly would be a sight, certainly a step up from Santa in a chopper. We had practiced with the animals for two days, adjusting them to the platform, the lights, even the choir. We had prepared for everything—except human stupidity.

The violin section warbled the solemn introduction as the shepherds and kings proceeded onto the podium. The audience gasped, especially at the sight of the camel. Beth looked stoic, rocking the cradle that held our plastic baby Jesus. Everything was fine until Walter Gillespie, King No. 1, decided to get off the camel, something we had not rehearsed. He struggled to dismount, trying to keep his costume in place while holding the box of gold. As he brought his right leg over the hump, the box slowly slid out of his hands. Always meticulous to detail, Mr. Mayes had placed three hundred spray-painted washers in the box, just in case it should be opened for some reason. Unfortunately, no one thought to lock the box.

Before the box crashed to the floor, the washers rained on the platform, scaring the animals and distracting the choir below. The choir missed a few notes and the animals stirred. The temperamental sheep who had previously bitten the elf, bounced around the platform like a pinball, finally crashing into the cradle. Before Beth could grab it, the cradle was airborne. I watched as the cradle and the baby Jesus separated, the cradle flying right, the doll flying left. When the cradle landed, it broke in half. The baby Jesus bounced a few times before resting at the choir director's feet. Luckily, the Lord and Savior didn't land in the grand piano.

The term "visual extravaganza" took on new meaning. The audience howled, the orchestra looked bewildered, the choir was pissed, the shepherds and kings calmed the animals and Mr. Mayes searched for a rope to hang himself with.

Amidst the chaos stood Beth, ever the picture of poise, always the actress.

Ignoring the pandemonium around her, she gracefully descended from the platform and retrieved the baby Jesus. She stood there, cradling the plastic doll as if it were her own child. Gradually the audience was drawn to the Madonna and the laughter subsided. When the solemnity of the moment was regained, Beth held the child skyward and said, "For unto you a child is born, Jesus Christ!"

A man clapped. Then someone else joined him.

The applause grew until it transformed into a standing ovation. The elves and dancers ran onto the stage (even a revived Wendy) and the entire company took a bow, Beth at the center, beaming, inebriated by the magic of applause.

January 22, 1982

Dear Sis,
I must admit that there are moments of profound levity staying here at the VA. A number of patients are regulars at our unit and it is from this select few that my favorites are fertilized. For one, there is Przbeweczki, who is convinced that the correct pronunciation of his name is Oswego. This is the very least of his problems.

And there is my friend Pepe who is an old tecato from the Barrio Viejo. Last week Pepe was at home pursuing his favorite pastimes—shooting dope and making dirty phone calls. One lady didn't hang up on him like most of them instinctually do. She even arranged for him to call her again the following afternoon. Unbeknownst to our hero, his newly discovered girlfriend was married to a cop. They had the phone rigged for a fast tracer and poor Pepe was still talking to the woman when the vice cops kicked his door down and cuffed him. They gave him his rights, took him downtown, booked him and permitted him to call a lawyer. Pepe used his one phone call to ring up the same woman and continue to talk dirty.

And there is Domingo, who is convinced that he is a Mafia don, when he is conscious, which is not nearly enough of the time, as far as Domingo is concerned. He doesn't like his medication. Doctor Chandrup, a psychiatrist from India, who attributes most psychotic reactions to a lack of sea sponge in the American diet, hates it when Domingo is off his meds. When he's on them, he is as exciting as watching laundry dry. But when he's off them, he likes to sneak up behind Dr. Chandrup and shout, "BANG!" in his ear. Drives the doctor nuts.

Such is life here at the VA, although I do miss my old life, and I can't say that it has been easy living without scotch. However, the doctors have made it clear that liquor and I must have a parting of the ways or my liver, and the triple bypass it received, will divorce me, if that's possible for an internal organ.

Looking forward to seeing you soon,
Charlie

Present Day

Screams of laughter carry through the patio door as Luke's blindfolded friend attempts to break the piñata dangling from our tangerine tree. The other guests stand a safe distance away, Sarah and my dad working crowd control while my brother manipulates the piñata string up and down, just giving each assaulter enough accurate swings to massage his ego and keep the piñata horse intact until all of the children have had a turn.

I kneel in front of my mother, watching the action from inside, where the air conditioning can control her body temperature.

"Why can't I go outside?" she asks for the fourth time.

"It's too hot, Mom. The kids will be back in after the piñata. You're not really missing much of the party," I add, knowing that she hates to be away from Luke and adores his company.

"Whose birthday is this anyway?" She is perturbed by either her forgetfulness or the boredom she faces sitting here in isolation.

"Mom, it's Luke's birthday. Your grandson." I pray that she remembers him when the children come inside. Luke will be devastated to think that his grandmother has forgotten him on his special day.

"Yes," is the simple reply. We sit in silence, watching the activity. I notice that like me, my mother can't help but smile at the children, lost in their glee, waiting in anticipation for the blow that will scatter the candy over the lawn.

Whether it is Luke's prowess for baseball or my brother's favoritism, his first swing crushes one of the horse's legs. Children dive for the candy and my mother laughs heartily, clapping her hands in excitement. While the children fill their bags, I wheel Mom to the dining room table and prepare the cake, knowing that the key to a successful birthday party is the constant flow of activity. Down time equals mischievousness.

The doorbell rings and I glance at the clock. We still have forty minutes of party time left, so I wonder if there are some parents who have exhausted their errands early. Instead I find two men dressed in white shirts and black pants—Mormon missionaries.

"Hello," the taller boy begins. "We're members of the Church of Jesus Christ of Latter Day Saints and we would like a few moments of your time."

Luke throws open the patio door and screams fill the air. The young men don't seem to notice the raucous laughter behind me. They continue to stand there with pleasant looks on their faces. As good Mormons, I know it will only be a matter of a few years before they portray the role of harried birthday party hosts. I need to cut them off quickly.

"Guys, I'm really busy right now, you know, doing the parent thing?" They nod sympathetically but they do not retreat, obviously well trained in missionary school not to be easily dismissed. "Besides, have you changed your opinions about gays in your church or gay marriage?" They look at each other uncomfortably. Missionary school clearly did not cover that question. "See, that would really cinch it for me and my wife."

One young man swallows hard and the other just shakes his head no.

"Didn't think so," I comment, before I shut the door.

Luke runs up to me. "Look, Mom!" he cries, holding up a very full bag of treats. "I got a ton!"

Soon all of the other children are comparing their loot and I realize that the adults have taken care to ensure that each child has about the same amount. When the children see the cake and presents, their bags are forgotten and they crowd around the table. A flurry of color and sound consumes the next twenty minutes, as Luke rips the colorful wrapping from his packages, party favor horns squawk endlessly and green dinosaur cake is inhaled by all.

Amidst the endless chatter of the children admiring Luke's gifts, Sarah wraps her arms around me and whispers in my ear. "Your dad offered to take Luke tonight." She kisses the back of my neck and I shiver.

"Hmm," I ponder. "What will we do with ourselves?"

As experienced hosts, we have adeptly timed the events and soon the doorbell is ringing and parents are claiming their sugar-high children who are still blowing their horns and stuffing their faces with piñata candy. All of the parents look unhappy that the party has ended and they are inheriting small whirling dervishes who have replaced the well-mannered children they dropped off two hours before. As calm is restored, the house echoes in quiet once the guests have departed. Luke disappears into his room, carrying his gifts, leaving the adults to clean up.

"Well, that was a great party," my mother states. "Who was it for?" she asks again.

"This was Luke's birthday, Mom," my brother states in a disappointed voice. He recognizes our mother is sundowning, a memory lapse condition that occurs in the late afternoon when her brain is tired.

My mother looks around at the dining room and she swings her head toward the den. "Why are we having it here? Whose house is this?"

"It's mine and Sarah's, Mom," I remind her.

"No it's not," she says, shaking her head. "I've never been to this house in my life."

"Well, we've lived here five years." I glance at Sarah, who is stacking dishes into the dishwasher.

"This isn't your house," she repeats. "I don't know why we're here but somebody's going to be in trouble."

My father pats her arm. "It's okay, honey. The girls own this place. They live here with Luke."

My mother's expression sours. "Where's Luke's father? Why does he live here with two women?"

I feel my stomach knot. Although we have stumbled upon this topic by accident, it is a historical sore spot between me and my mother and while she can no longer remember the endless debates that raged throughout my parents' house about my lesbianism, there is nothing wrong with my memory and her comments sting.

"Kate was artificially inseminated," my brother explains patiently. He was too young to remember my coming out and he is only trying to help now, not recognizing that he should just let the topic drop. "Luke doesn't have a father in the normal sense, Mom. You know all this. You were there when Luke was born."

"No, I wasn't." My mother turns and glares at me. "Luke should have a father."

"I'll go see if I can find one in the phone book," I answer dryly.

"Don't be smart with me, missy," she scolds. "The Bible is very clear about the sin of homosexuality."

My anger is surfacing, overriding my pity for my mother's condition, as a flash from an ancient argument breaks the surface of time. I want to scream at her, *We worked all this out years ago! Don't you remember?* I breathe deeply and take the remaining dishes into the kitchen.

"You okay?" Sarah whispers.

"Yeah."

"She can't help it, honey."

"I know."

My father and brother strap my mother into her wheelchair and check her oxygen. It is clearly a good time to make an exit. I gather some of Luke's things together while my brother loads my mother into the car. She is quiet, unwilling to give either Sarah or myself a hug good-bye. We watch the car drive away, Luke waving at us from the back window, acting as though he is a prisoner being kidnapped. Sarah and I laugh and the mood lightens.

"I'm going for a walk," I decide.

I retrieve the dog's leash and Dash our Labrador immediately appears. He knows our route and needs little direction from me. I put the day out of my mind as we stroll around the nearby park, me lost in my thoughts while Dash marks every tree in sight. I try to think of nothing except Luke and Sarah, avoiding thoughts of my mother and especially the memories from the past about the most difficult time of my life.

Creatures of habit, once we have made our circle we return home, exactly forty-five minutes later than when we left. The house is dark and Sarah has turned on some jazz. I make my way into our bedroom, which is illuminated by several candles. I hear a splash and open the door to the bathroom, more candlelight casting shadows around the room, Sarah's face ensconced in the glow. She rests in the bathtub, surrounded by bubbles, holding a glass of wine. I notice another full glass waits on the counter.

"Get in," she commands.

I start to undress, a smile creeping on to my face. "You know, my mother wouldn't approve."

Sarah shakes her head. "I'm not going there, Kate. You need to remember how much she loves you and how happy she was the day we got married. The past is the past and she's technically gone, at least her mind is. How much she has ever approved of our relationship, well, we'll never know and it's just not that important. Now, if you don't get into this bathtub, and stop thinking about your mother, I'm going to get really pissed."

Years of being together tell me I should do exactly what she says. I slide in front of her, letting her embrace me, touch me. Once the wine is drained, we explore each other with the familiarity of old lovers.

I moan when Sarah's fingers enter me. "Do you love me?" she asks, her voice thick, her mouth pulling at my earlobe.

"I adore you."

She transports me to places that are far away, free of my mind, relying only on my most primitive urges and needs. If our love is evil or unnatural, it is at least compassionate, allowing me to forget the many other roles I play in my life. For the first time today, I am not a mother, wife, sister, daughter, friend, caretaker, agnostic, patriot, party planner, dog owner, consumer, teacher or Alzheimer's advocate.

For the first time all day, I finally define myself as my harshest critics believe I do every minute—as a lesbian.

Birthday Surprises

"My parents are forcing me to go to the prom," Beth announced as she slammed her locker door shut.

"How do your parents force you to go to the prom?" I asked.

She sighed. "Kate, c'mon."

She was right. I knew the answer to that question. I'd heard it before the country club formal, the debutante ball, and now the Valley High junior-senior prom.

When it came to discussions about philosophical issues or her teenage behavior, Beth could fight with her parents better than most of my peers but as strong a person as she was, Beth couldn't stand up to them when it came to social events that affected their status. Although Beth scowled whenever I mentioned anything concerning high society, she knew which fork to use with what course during a meal, how to waltz and various other rules of etiquette that were not commonplace to most high school seniors. She understood and accepted the role of a rich doctor's daughter, even if it meant attending stuffy, black-tie events with a BOY.

"I know you're disappointed but I have to go. James and I are going together, since he's getting as much pressure from *his* dad as I am from mine."

Our friend James was stuck with an unfortunate fortune—his father's multimillion dollar construction company and, like Beth, James knew the rules of the wealthy. Although James had no intention of ever picking up a hammer or unrolling a set of blueprints, he appreciated the other benefits of the construction industry—namely sweaty, tanned hunks in tight jeans. He'd managed to date all of the gay men on his father's payroll and he was now working his way through all of the subcontractors who floated in and out of the job sites.

"I thought James and Reynoldo were going away that weekend." Reynoldo was James's latest boyfriend.

"No," Beth said, shaking her head. "James's dad freaked when he found out James was going to skip the prom." She haughtily threw her sweater over her shoulders. "Got to protect the big *I*," she said mockingly.

The big "I" was our code for image, a word frequently associated with teenagers but actually more appropriate for rich adults.

"Well that just sucks," I said, leaning against the lockers. "I thought we were going to get to be together, kind of have our own prom. You know, for my birthday?"

Beth wiped away a tear, knowing she was breaking a promise to me. She had said she would plan a fabulous evening for the two of us, but clearly her familial obligations came first. "You know I don't want to go. I'm just doing this for my dad, Kate. You know that." The thirty-second warning bell sounded, signifying the beginning of the school day. The halls cleared and we stood in silence, neither one of us ready to go to class until this was resolved.

"Hey," Beth exclaimed, "why don't you take Reynoldo?"

"Are you crazy? I'd rather tell my parents I'm gay than try and explain why I'm taking a twenty-seven-year-old man to the prom!"

"When are you going to tell them about us?" Beth asked, changing the subject.

"About the time you tell your folks," I retorted.

She shook her head and waved her hand for a truce. "We're not getting anywhere, Kate. Let's talk about this after school." She dashed off toward her first period leaving me to stew about our fight, the prospect of spending prom night alone and most importantly, my dilemma with my parents.

We were very close but they were in the dark about that one little detail of my life. Uncle Charlie had kept his promise, although he constantly harped and suggested I leave the closet. He'd even gone so far as to send me a broom for Christmas last year hoping I'd take the hint. I couldn't wait to see what he got me for my birthday.

For the next few weeks everyone bothered me. Beth would switch from being the understanding girlfriend to the frustrated daughter who expected me to sympathize with her situation. My parents probed and questioned me about my prom prospects every night at dinner. My softball team wasn't happy that my pitching was slumping and my trigonometry grade was in the toilet. I was just trying to ride out the wave, hoping that life would improve after prom and my birthday, which I wasn't looking forward to at all.

The day of my birthday, I arrived home to find a package sitting on the hallway table. From the scribbling on the cover I knew it was a book and I knew it was from my uncle. I tore off the brown mailing paper and found a small collection of American poetry. I thumbed through it, a flash of green catching my eye. I turned back to the spot and found a twenty dollar bill. Across the bottom of the bill Uncle Charlie had written, *Kate, I hope you know what to do with both of these.* My eyes shifted from the money to the poem on the open page. "Richard Cory" by E.A. Robinson. It took a few seconds for Consuela Consuela's prophecy to register.

Before my mother could come by and question me about the gift, I hurried up to my room to read about Richard Cory. He was a well-bred man that everyone assumed was perfectly happy. Emotionally, though, he was tortured. Mr. Robinson never stated what was destroying Richard but in the end he killed himself.

I forgot about the prom and Beth. My mind was consumed with Richard Cory. Did my uncle really think I would destroy myself if I didn't tell my parents I was gay? Beth's parents didn't know. James's parents *certainly* didn't know. A lot of gay children never told their parents. What was the big deal?

"Kate?"

I awoke from my daze staring at my dinner plate. Most of my birthday dinner was gone and I couldn't remember eating it. "Yeah?"

"Honey, Grandma just asked you what Uncle Charlie sent you for your birthday." I turned to see Grandma's amused smile. She knew I was out in the ozone. I couldn't remember the last three hours at all.

"He gave me a book of poetry."

Grandma snorted. "Poetry? Why the hell did he give you that? You hate poetry."

I blushed. "Maybe he forgot."

Grandma pointed her corncob in my direction. "Forgot? Your uncle has never forgotten anything. His damn memory has taken years off of my life. So spill it, Kate. Why'd he get you the book?"

I looked at my family. They all stared at me. It would have been easy to lie. It would have just been another small and insignificant untruth that I regularly told my parents to avoid the truth. I could create these white lies without thought—I'd been doing it most of my life. Every time they asked me about boys, Beth, my future and especially sex, I conveniently changed the subject.

"He gave me that book of poetry because there's a poem included called 'Richard Cory'."

My father and grandmother looked at my puzzled mom, the former teacher. "Why would he want you to read that?" she asked.

"Who was Richard Cory?" my little sister, Karen, asked.

"He was suicidal over his life," my father summarized. "Kate, is there something we need to talk about?"

"Kate, you're not on drugs, are you?"

"No, Mom. It's nothing like that."

"Then what's wrong?" my father asked gently.

"I'm gay."

The room was silent for several seconds, even my younger siblings recognizing that I had made an important declaration, although they had no idea what. I waited for my parents' reaction but it was Grandma who broke the silence.

"Are we having birthday cake? I'm still hungry."

I glanced at my grandmother and smiled. God, I loved her.

Then my mother started to laugh. It wasn't a side-splitting, wise-cracking laugh, but the kind of nervous laughter that one chooses over wailing sobs. "Kate, honey, is this some kind of joke?"

I could only shake my head.

"Oh, my," she said with a smile. She turned to my father, who remained expressionless. "I'm not sure where we've gone wrong, Joe, but I'm pretty sure our Hawaii fund just got reassigned to counseling for our daughter."

I was shocked. "Mom, I'm gay, I'm not mentally ill! This isn't some kind of disease. It's just who I am."

"Who you are? And how do you know who you are? You just turned seventeen. No one knows who they are then and besides, you've only had one boyfriend in your whole life! How do you know you don't like boys?"

"I just know," I said.

Her eyes narrowed and I knew she was analyzing the last year of my life, deciding when the moment occurred that I gave up on men. "It's Beth, isn't it?"

"What do you mean?" I asked stupidly.

"She's turned you into a lesbian, hasn't she?"

"She hasn't turned me into anything!" I yelled. "This isn't about anyone but me!"

My mother snorted. "It most certainly is, young lady. I'd say this has a lot to do with your father and me, as well. You're a part of this family, so we're all affected."

"Do you mean your precious reputation as a school board member or your position as my mother?"

Her cheeks turned crimson and she stood. "How dare you, young lady! How dare you!" She stormed out of the room, as my sister started to cry and ran to follow her. My brother kept eating, avoiding the entire ordeal, and my father just stared at me.

"I think I'd better go check on your mother," he mumbled.

I closed my eyes, replaying my mother's reaction, the sting of each word cutting into my heart. I started to cry and Grandma handed me her napkin. She didn't say anything but she just patted my knee, waiting for me to finish.

When I'd exhausted my tears, she rose and took my plate. "Help me with the dishes," she said.

I followed her into the kitchen and we loaded the dishwasher in silence. She filled the sink with soapsuds and pots, motioning to me to take the dishtowel.

"Kate, have you ever heard of the Cotton Club?"

"Not really," I said absently.

"It was a nightclub in Harlem during the Twenties and even though it was in Harlem, a lot of white people went there too."

"I didn't know that," I said, trying to be polite but not really caring. I just wanted to get out of the house but if anyone deserved my respectful attention, I knew it was Grandma.

"Oh, yes. It was the best dance spot in all of New York. At least, that's my opinion."

"I'd forgotten you lived in New York."

"Uh-hum. From Twenty-nine to Thirty-two. All the biggies used to go there, straight and gay. Bessie Smith, Joan Crawford, lots of people."

"Joan Crawford was gay?"

"Joan Crawford was bisexual, at least I think that's the term they use now."

"How do you know?"

"Because I do."

"Grandma, what are you saying?"

"What do you think? I know for a fact that Joan Crawford slept with women."

I managed to set my mother's china serving bowl on the counter before it slipped through my fingers and crashed to the floor. "Grandma, what about Grandpa?"

She chuckled and dried her hands on a dishrag. "Oh, this was several years before I met your grandfather. I was barely older than you are now. I was spreading my wings. Experimenting."

"With Joan Crawford?" I really couldn't believe this.

"Among others."

"So eventually you decided you weren't attracted to women and you met Grandpa and that was it."

She smiled at my attempt to reassemble the world she'd just shattered. "It wasn't quite that simple. You may find this hard to believe, Kate, but I had a scandalous youth."

"Grandma, I don't doubt it one bit. So tell me what happened between you and Joan Crawford?"

"Nothing ever became of it. One-night stand. Later, I realized I liked men as much as women, so I chose to be with men. You see, it was easier that way. Homosexuality was a taboo, especially amongst women. When a woman was discovered to be a homosexual, she was shunned, abandoned, sometimes even put into a mental institution."

"Doesn't sound like too much has changed," I added.

"Well, it's better but you're right. There's still a long way to go."

"So to avoid all that, you just gave up on women?"

"Yep. It just didn't make sense to get everything all stirred up when it really didn't matter to me all that much. But you see I was one of the lucky ones. Some of the girls didn't want to be intimate with any man. Some of the girls were like you." She looked up and smiled a warm smile that erased my immediate embarrassment.

"Uncle Charlie figured it out, you know."

She chuckled. "He is a different kind of person. Never judges anyone. Nothing or nobody ever surprises him, bless his heart." Her smile was full of love and she took my hand. "Your mother is the night to your uncle's day. She's a straight arrow and this is going to take her some time to understand but she will, honey, *she will*."

"Does she know about you?"

Grandma laughed. "Oh, no! Your mother would have heart failure if she knew. You see, Kate, as children grow up, they develop ideas and images of their parents. They see them in certain ways. It's too late for me to share this with your mother. She'd feel betrayed and she'd question my relationship with your grandfather. Instead of sending you to college we'd have to put your mother in therapy."

We finished the dishes in silence and I drove her back to her retirement village, making a pit stop at the local Dairy Queen for a birthday sundae. We talked about other things, the gossip at bingo night, her continuing romance with Bernard Rock and what I wanted to do with my life.

When I pulled up to her duplex, she turned and faced me, a wicked smile on her face. "So Kate, are you screwing Beth?"

"Grandma! I can't believe the things you say sometimes. You have such a dirty mind."

Grandma chuckled. "Impossible, honey. There are very few advantages to being over sixty-five but one of them is that you can get away with practically anything. Thirty years ago I had a dirty mind. Now I just don't know what I'm saying."

"That's bullshit, Grandma."

"Yeah, honey, it is, but so is growing old."

June 2, 1982

Sister Mine,

I am once more ensconced in my wee apartment, free from the sleepless nights of Ward Six and the endless rounds of guilt-edged therapy sessions. While I am ever in danger of slipping, I have learned a number of things I can do to temper my occasional fits of thirst. They all involve various methods of relaxation and self-control, but in extreme cases, one can always rely on good old fashioned Pavlovian fear. The doctors have told me quite simply: You drink, you die. Hard words to an alcoholic.

Another thing that helps me stay sober is the knowledge that I have one hellavalot more friends than what I ever suspected. Yet another tool for maintaining sobriety has been suggested to me by one of my doctors. He flatly recommended the use of marijuana. A second doctor did not recommend it, but he had no strong objection to it. The third doctor hadn't the faintest idea what I was talking about. He said he wouldn't mind trying some.

I have managed to keep my head above the financial waterline these past three months. I still have to figure out my income taxes but that shouldn't be such a problem since I now give the mess over to a professional. I tried doing my own taxes for the last time in 1976, using what was deceptively called the "simple form." It drove me bananas and I got heinously drunk and ended up eating my W-2 forms. You might be interested to know that W-2 forms are a natural emetic.

I don't worry a bit about recuperating. Tucson Medical Center says they aren't quite through tabulating my bill, but so far it looks like it will break the $127,000 mark. This doesn't even begin to include what the doctors are going to want. I am going to ask my boss at KTJP if we can hold a telethon for me. One item on the bill I intend to contest. They say I owe them $6,676 for "drugs." I don't remember getting off once while I was there.

The doctor still has not given me permission to return to work as yet, but I stop by the studio every so often to keep abreast of things and try to peek down Carla's blouse. I even gave our crack news department a top-dog story. I have proof that Pope John Paul was forced by the College of Cardinals to reject the name he originally wanted. They insisted he shorten it. He wanted to be known as Pope John Paul Ringo and George, but they wouldn't buy it.

That's about all to report for now, my love. I think I will be calling Mom before too long. In the meantime, I will lay down and listen to myself gurgle. It is very good to be among the living once again, no matter for how long.

Charlie

The Journal

Moonlight swept through the cracks of the clapboard tree house, washing over us, a balance of shadow and light that created a serenely romantic mood. After an hour of fabulous sex, followed by a huge bout of the giggles over the ecstasy of completing our junior year exams, we were still. We lay in each other's arms on the old mattress, whispering, sharing the intimate secrets we told no one else and would never remember years later. My hand gently caressed the incredible curve of Beth's hip and I knew it wouldn't take long for me to be completely aroused once more.

She smiled and I sucked in my breath at her beauty. I concentrated on her face, mesmerized by the honey gold flecks of her eyes, realizing I had never stared so intently at her, knowing we wouldn't see each other for the entire summer.

"What time does your flight leave tomorrow?" The disappointment in my voice was apparent.

"Nine." She closed her eyes and pressed against me. "You know I don't really want to go."

"Yes, you do," I chuckled.

"Well, it is an incredible opportunity. Not that many high school students are allowed to participate."

"You got in because you're so talented," I replied, kissing the top of her head. "And you're getting to go because your parents want us apart," I added truthfully.

My coming out generated continuous explosions in my house and forced Beth to admit the truth to her own parents once my mother assuaged her conscience by sharing my news with Mr. and Mrs. Simms, since she held Beth responsible for my lesbianism. Allowing Beth to remain in the closet was unjust in my mother's opinion, since Beth's predatory instincts would eventually overcome her and another helpless heterosexual would be converted. She decided it was her duty to inform Beth's parents about what was really going on in the tree house.

Upon learning their daughter was gay, Beth's parents had offered words of support and encouragement. They had also sprung for a summer drama workshop in New York at an arts school and were already gathering brochures from theatre programs in California, realizing that if Beth attended the University of Arizona, there was a much greater likelihood that we would remain lovers after graduation next year. They were as upset and disgusted as my parents but their passive-aggressive nature, combined with their country club gentility, wouldn't allow them to fight overtly with Beth. Instead of shaking the walls with shouting matches as my family did, they merely found an atlas and a phone book and started making plans. The joke, however, was really on them since we'd decided long ago that our relationship ended with the beginning of college. We had begun as friends and we would remain friends.

"Are you taking summer school?" she asked into my chest.

"Yeah. I'll do anything to stay out of the house. My mom and I are not getting along."

Beth brought her head up and looked at me compassionately. "She'll come around, Kate, I know it. Your mom is incredible."

"My mom is Catholic," I stated. "And I am a sinner. She loves me but she hates my choices." I mimicked my mother's tone perfectly, except for the disdain that filled my voice. She had made her declaration during our last family dinner the week before, the last time we had spoken.

The family dinner my parents coveted during my early youth eventually gave way to Boy Scouts for my brother, dance recitals for my sister, play rehearsals for me and for my mother, the endless commitments of a school board member aspiring to become a legislator. Our time together dwindled to ninety minutes of mandated mastication every Sunday, as my mother attempted to preserve the framework of the nuclear family she had created. Although the actors appeared in this drama each week, since the announcement of my sexuality, the dialogue was sorely lacking in substance. My teenage siblings could only carry dinner conversation so far, regarding their sheltered lives and the trivial issues they faced and my mother couldn't look at me, except to make a request to pass a bowl or plate of food. My father played the peacemaker, clearly pained by the huge division that separated his wife and eldest child. About once a month he would attempt to bridge the gaping chasm between us by introducing a topic we heartily agreed upon—hatred of Ronald Reagan's presidency.

"I just can't believe anyone would buy into Reagonomics," my father interjected, having heard enough of my brother's atrocious cafeteria stories involving chewed peas, the ceiling and straws.

I nodded my agreement. "My history teacher says that anyone who thinks money is going to trickle down from the wealthy to the middle class doesn't understand how the wealthy *stay* wealthy."

"Oh, they'll throw some of it back into the economy," my mother commented, "but not nearly as much as they'll keep for themselves."

We all nodded and my father seemed rather pleased with himself. My mother and I had spoken words, granted, not to each other directly, but the tone and choice were cordial. This was progress.

Ever looking for opportunities to discuss my growing understanding of the subculture I had embraced, I sought moments to discuss gay topics, however uncomfortable it might make my audience, including my mother. "You know, President Reagan is also responsible for the spread of this new disease."

My mother shook her head. "What do you mean?"

"Well, they say he's not doing anything about it because it's only infecting gay men in San Francisco right now but a lot of people are saying that it could kill straight people too."

I gauged my parents' reaction. My facts were limited partly because I was not as informed as I could have been since I rarely read a newspaper anymore, and also because my source of information, James, wasn't very reliable.

"I don't know about that, honey," my mother countered. "It's awfully hard to blame one man for the lack of morals that a group of people display."

My mother's voice dripped with judgment and my father's face cracked in half. I'd pushed an issue and destroyed the peace.

"Do you mean gay people aren't moral?"

My mother took a deep breath and sipped her wine before answering. "I mean that if people choose to have random sex with multiple partners, then there will be risks."

I leaned over my plate, pointing my fork at her. "That's easy to say but if no one educates people, then there can't be any prevention." I looked at my father for support but he was not choosing sides, eating his pork chop silently like any good Switzerland would.

"That's a good point," my mother conceded, attempting to be diplomatic. "On another note, Kate, have you decided what you'll wear for the family photo for my candidacy?"

I shrugged my shoulders in indifference. The idea that my face would be plastered on street signs all over legislative District 20 was not something I relished, although secretly I was proud of my mother.

"I don't know. Probably just some nice pants and a shirt."

"I could take you shopping?" she suggested. "We could find something nice?"

She asked it as a question but the weight hung behind her words. This was a chance to create a manufactured occasion that would require me to wear a dress or a skirt. I could have dismissed her offer pleasantly without rebuke, but maturity was like the bottle of wine that sat before my mother—both required proper aging, something I still lacked.

"Mom, I'm not wearing a dress or a skirt! You need to just forget that right now. If your constituents figure out that you've got a gay daughter, well, that's not my problem!"

"That's not what I was getting at—"

"Like hell it wasn't!" I shot back. "You want to get me out to a mall so you can guilt me into wearing some feminine *het* outfit, probably with makeup, so you'll look good in front of the voters."

"What's a het?" Tommy asked.

"A het-er-o-sex-u-al," I answered acidly.

My mother broiled in her chair. She was stiff, unable to speak, unwilling to lose control. When she finally looked at me, her face was expressionless, an empty room.

"That was extremely cruel, Kate. And if being a lesbian means you've sacrificed all of your good manners and common decency, then I'm really against it."

"As if you'd ever be for it anyway," I muttered.

"That's enough." My father's sharp voice was a rare occurrence but he possessed a head of household tone that ended conversations and cast the definitive opinion.

"No, Joe," my mother disagreed. Her voice was quivering and I could see the bundle of energy rising through her body. She'd obviously planned what she was going to say and there was nothing that could hold it back. "Kate, I don't approve of your choices, the religious implications aside. You'll have to take up that part with God. You know I've always tried to teach you tolerance and I intend to practice what I preach. You are my daughter and I will always love you, even if I don't understand. Even if I don't agree. I can't tell you that it doesn't matter, because it does. It's as if I don't know you."

The words were nothing new, many of them recycled sound bites from arguments we'd endured for weeks. What was different, though, was my mother's tone and it made me laugh.

"I'm glad you think it's so funny," my mother retorted.

"I'm having a moment of déjà vu," I said. "From third grade."

Both of my parents looked perplexed and my mother narrowed her eyes, certain a caustic remark was forming on my lips.

"I'm remembering the time I cheated on my math test in Mrs. Angle's class. When we talked about it, you sounded exactly the way you do now."

My mother's face crumbled at the realization and the symbolism of that incident, the only time in my life my parents had been ashamed of me.

"You must think quite a bit less of me," she whispered. "And if I'm honest with myself," she continued, finally looking up at me, "if I'm honest, I think quite a bit less of you."

The truth of disapproval drifted to the center of the dining room table, the place where all familial truths are eventually aired, and stayed there for many years, unanswered and unacknowledged.

"Kate?" Beth called.

She had slipped from my arms and was busily gathering her clothes. I watched her cover the beautiful tanned shoulders I loved to kiss and the long legs I'd admired since junior high.

"I need to go pack," she stated without emotion.

I dressed and we descended the tree house ladder. I glanced up at the rickety old boards resting between the branches, conduits of support. I remembered the summer Mr. Simms had erected the tree house for his children and I was certain he would be out in the yard with a crowbar immediately after Beth's flight departed tomorrow, now that he knew we had converted it from friendly clubhouse to sex den.

She kissed me quickly on the cheek, mumbled an "I love you" and disappeared into the house.

Beth's departure voided a layer of my personality, one that needed her presence to exist. I found it impossible to be a lesbian without her, as her ego defined and gave the shape and contour to my own. While I would never admit it to my mother, without Beth I had no idea what being a lesbian meant and since my sexuality was the only aspect of my personality that seemed to matter to my parents, I chose to stay away from them as much as possible.

By the second week of summer it was evident I could avoid my mother for approximately twenty-three hours and fifty-five minutes of each day. The five minutes we inhabited the same space, usually the kitchen, was a ballet of avoidance, both of us furtively moving between the necessary appliances we used. The hum of the refrigerator, the gurgling of the coffee pot or the beeping of our new microwave provided the only sounds and punctuated the loneliness we both felt for the past, when the kitchen was a place for discussion and emotion, a time when my mother and I were friends.

I spent my day as a nomad—working, studying and playing. My job as a lifeguard at the community pool afforded me a summer of gazing at beautiful women in bathing suits and the fantasy of administering mouth to mouth to any one of them. I could have eaten at the snack bar and avoided my mother entirely if I had not been disgusted by the continent of cockroaches that shared the cabinets with the candy, hot dogs and nachos.

My parents tacitly accepted my absence, never questioning why I would leave as the sun came up and not return until the bars closed. Although I loved going to the gay bars with James and the fake ID he'd helped me acquire, I was, in fact, terrified. Many of the buildings looked abandoned, decrepit afterthoughts with little maintenance, located on streets I'd never driven down during my sheltered life in suburbia. The bars were small, uninviting and generally claustrophobic testaments to the shame felt by the gay community. Built to go unnoticed, the bars of the Eighties provided safety for their anonymous patrons who flaunted their sexuality only when the sun disappeared but displayed their chameleon skin in their workplaces the next day.

The highlight of my life proved to be summer school. Determined to earn college credits, I enrolled in English 101 at Phoenix College, believing that my straight A's in high school validated my prowess with language. Within three class meetings I was greatly humbled and the breadth of my ignorance was clearly obvious to me and my grad student teacher, Ms. Roxanne Case.

When she walked in that first morning, a tall, striking blond wearing a conservative suit, she announced, "I'm Ms. Roxanne Case and we're here to write." The tone was immediately set and we knew there would be no first name camaraderie, she would not wear hot tank tops or low-cut jeans and we would never be invited to have a beer after class with the good looking grad student. We would work and she would grade.

"Hopefully, you've all done the pre-reading so you won't be behind," she continued. I glanced at the nervous expressions of my mostly older classmates and I drew the same conclusions with Ms. Case. "I take it that the majority of the class is unprepared? Don't let that happen again."

We all watched as she packed up her briefcase and walked out.

I was in awe of her and her fabulous calves. She lived on a different plane, aloof from the petty antics of collegiate life and the general laziness that engulfed so many professors who were distraught and perturbed with any student that visited them during established office hours. Ms. Case fascinated me and I desperately wanted to please her, but my diligence failed to translate into exceptional grades. By the third week, I was expecting the red swirls and comments that littered my essay on the Underground Railroad, a topic I had thoroughly researched. I was surprised, though, when she wrote, "Do you really care about this?" at the top of my paper, next to the bloating C-minus that rested above the first line.

"Just drop the class," James advised later that night as we hit our favorite club. "She's obviously some power hungry bitch. Or maybe she hates lesbians."

The music at The Back Pocket swelled and James pulled me to the dance floor, halting our conversation. I let the music and the women erase my memory of the class, concentrating on understanding my personal life, and the feelings that raced through my body any time a woman sidled up to me, often cutting in on James and following my moves. Some would smile seductively as our eyes met while others wrapped their arms around me, causing my body to shake with terror at my inexperience and ignorance. I was only a lesbian with Beth. The handbook I followed was very short, only one chapter long. I didn't know the rules and I had no idea what to do with a woman who was genuinely interested me.

A year before I would have asked my mother for help with all of my problems, or Beth or my uncle. Now they had all exited my life in one way or another, including my Uncle Charlie, who had returned to the hospital. He had quit drinking but perhaps not soon enough.

Resigned to accepting James's advice and forfeiting the tuition, I lingered after class one day, waiting until the room cleared and Ms. Case was gathering her papers.

"Is there something you need, Miss Mitchell?"

I stuck my hands in my pockets, kicking myself for not practicing my speech. She rose to her full height, her back ramrod straight, briefcase in hand.

"Um, well, I just wanted to tell you that I'm probably going to drop the class."

An eyebrow raised and the flicker of concern passed over her eyes. "Why?" She tossed the briefcase down and leaned back against the desk, preparing for a longer discussion.

A wave of regret and understanding overtook me and I couldn't look at her. Suddenly this was about so much more than a C-minus. "I don't have time," I said meekly. Neither one of us believed my lame explanation, of this I was sure.

I knew she was staring but I could only drag my eyes across the long grains of the oak teacher's desk.

"I see. Would this decision have anything to do with your grades thus far?"

I loved her use of proper English. She wasn't trying to show off. She had a solid grasp of the language and had no intention of watering down her speech for anyone, even if she sounded patronizing.

Did it have anything to do with my grade? Yes, and no, I thought. Everything and nothing. I stood there, mute and confused.

"Do you always quit when it gets hard?"

Fury brought a reaction, which was what she wanted. I opened my mouth to protest but she held up her hand and motioned for me to sit. I took a chair in the front row and she sat down beside me, her perfume invading my personal space, breaching the professional distance she'd established. I'd never been close enough to her to know she wore perfume and this one smelled heavenly.

"Kate, I want you to understand something. You're a wonderful writer. You're a wonderful writer who's afraid to write." I furrowed my brow and shook my head, not having the slightest idea what she meant. "You pick these topics that are removed from you. They're sterile. Safe. And while I feel my life has been enriched by knowing more about Harriet Tubman and the contribution she made as an abolitionist, I'm more interested in you and the contribution you'll make, especially since you're still living. I want to know about you, Kate. What's important to you and why you are the way you are? That's what you need to write about."

"I don't have anything to say," I offered. And I really didn't think I did.

"I can't believe that. I've listened to you participate and I know that any daughter of Barbara Mitchell, future state senator, must have a definite set of opinions."

I looked away at the mention of my mother's name, my stomach instantly churning, my expression lax.

"It seems as if we've hit upon a topic," she said softly.

"You want me to write about my relationship with my mother?"

"Only if you want to. I'm not trying to pry into your personal life, Kate, but I am asking you to assess your feelings about life and what's important to you."

She said many other things, but my head remained down, my eyes closed, listening to the gentle rhythm of her voice, like water flowing downstream. My thoughts drifted to my journal that was thrown haphazardly on my desk, its pages filled with vitriolic attacks on my mother, odes of gratitude to my understanding father and rather raunchy accounts of my sexual exploits with Beth.

It appeared to be just another composition book for one of my classes, nothing that my mother would ever notice during her secret explorations of my room that she thought I didn't know about. The cheap black cover telegraphed nothing of importance and I'd written WORLD HISTORY NOTES on the front, knowing my mother would never be interested in perusing such a dry and mundane topic. Hiding it in plain sight was genius on my part, because although she burrowed through my closets and between my mattresses looking for whatever nonexistent contraband she thought she would find, she rarely noticed anything within an arm's reach. A marijuana plant could have sat on the windowsill and she probably would have missed it.

That night, after my siblings were engrossed in *The Love Boat*, I stretched out on my bed and thumbed through my journal. My eyes darted to the bedroom door, certain my mother would charge into the room and my last thread of privacy would be destroyed. I knew I was being ridiculous, since my parents were at a neighbor's house, strategizing for the election that she was predicted to win.

Reading the entries was challenging as they were written haphazardly in random order, with no adherence to the parallel thin blue lines imprinted on the pages. Even the handwriting was different, based on mood swings and passion of subject. My normal, everyday writing possessed a lazy, round curvature. When I was upset, I composed in sharp, straight lines, like a connect-the-dots picture. There were a few drawings and designs scattered amongst the pages, mostly pictorial requiems of hatred against my mother. On one page I had outlined alternative slogans for her legislative campaigns—slogans such as, Vote for Barb: She'll Love Your Daughter More Than her Own! or Barbara Mitchell, The Homo Hater!

They weren't very good but they were venomous. I skimmed through many entries, my eyes catching only a few words on some pages and settling into whole paragraphs on others. Whether it was the memory behind the writing or the words themselves, I experienced a range of emotions with each passage I perused. I laughed when I remembered my uncle's last Christmas visit, where my grandmother and I tried our first joint. My teeth clenched as I read every word of an entry that recounted a fight with my mother over attending Oberlin, my college of choice and I cried when a small obituary notice slipped from between the pages and fell on the bed. Faded and yellowed, the five-year-old newsprint memorialized my former gym teacher, Miss Jones, who had become Mrs. Sawyer. After she had left our school under the cloud of controversy, she had married and had two children. When she had died of breast cancer, they were very young and I empathized with them, remembering how hurt I'd felt when Miss Jones had left me. I stared at the dark picture that accompanied the solemn words from her husband. My mother had shown her such compassion when no one else would, yet she ostracized and judged me harshly.

Then I remembered. Miss Jones really wasn't gay.

I slipped the clipping back between the pages and shut my journal, still without a topic, unwilling to share the raw nerves that drifted from my most personal secrets, my vulnerability. Anger surfaced. Anger at Ms. Case, whom I was now sure got her kicks from the pain and sorrow of her students, which she could transform into college gossip after the poor saps had prostrated their emotional baggage into a hard copy. I pictured her sitting amongst her graduate peers, a pitcher of margaritas between them, ridiculing the writing of those of us who feared a stark, blank sheet of paper.

I would drop the class.

I didn't bother to get up early the next day, since the registrar's office really didn't care if I arrived at the stroke of eight to withdraw. Loneliness met defeat at the doorway of my mind and I couldn't decide which bothered me more—admitting that I couldn't excel in an academic course or having no one to talk to about the doubt that eclipsed my decision. By nature I was not a quitter, stubborn in my beliefs, my actions a mirror of my intentions. I was easy to read, always a straight shooter. I was my mother and that was why she would someday be a celebrated state senator, her honesty and forthrightness craved by her constituents.

I wasn't even aware she was still home when I finally dragged myself into the kitchen at nine thirty. She was sitting at the breakfast bar, several documents in front of her, a cigarette between her fingers.

"What are you still doing here?" Her tone only conveyed surprise and perhaps a slight bit of concern. I watched as she stubbed out the cigarette and picked up a pen, ready to review the sheaf of papers in front of her.

"I'm not going to class today."

"Why? Did she cancel?"

I shook my head and busied myself with preparing a bagel. It seemed very important to me not to show weakness in front of my mother. Somehow this issue transcended all the others we fought about, particularly my sexuality. I was already less of a person in her eyes and to admit I wasn't going back, in a strange way, had a connection to our current struggles. It was complex and I certainly couldn't explain it.

"Kate, what's wrong?"

"Nothing," I said. "I just don't feel like going to class today."

"You haven't been down on school since Mrs. Angle's class," she observed. "You love education and your dad said you liked this grad student and thought she was good. So why would you skip?"

My mouth opened, preparing for sharp words to slice the distance between us but I caught them in a split second, the tone of my voice changing as my lips formed words. "I'm dropping the class."

"Can I ask why?"

This was the kindest, gentlest turn of phrase she had said to me in months. For the first time since I'd come out, my mother asked a question like a question and not a judgment veiled in concern. Instead of instantly hurling a snide retort back at her like a sailing boomerang, I took a breath and thought about the reasons.

"Honestly, I can't write what she wants. I can't open my soul and be all emotional. That's just not how I am and she doesn't want to read anything that isn't about me."

My mother suppressed a chuckle and sipped her coffee. "No, that's not you. There's nothing sappy about you, not at all. You're the only girl I've known who has *never* cried at a movie, who never spent middle school in a state of high drama and who has never traumatized over her wardrobe on a Monday morning, screaming for new clothes or sure that some boy would notice she'd worn the same thing the week before."

"And is my nonemotional attitude a problem?" I could feel my defenses rising. I knew it was too go to be true.

"Are you kidding? You saved me so much grief that I was able to deal with Karen! She has enough for both of you!"

We both laughed and it felt so good, even if it was at the expense of my genius IQ twelve-year-old sister who would inevitably attend an Ivy League school but never have the common sense to wait for a green light to cross the street.

"Do you remember the time Dad had to run out on Christmas Eve and hunt for a Barbie townhouse because Karen decided at the last minute she had to have it or she would die?" I asked.

My mother shook her head still laughing. "I told him to make her wait but we both knew she'd make a scene the next morning if it wasn't there. Your father has always had a soft spot for each of you and with Karen, it's always been about making her happy."

"And what do you think his soft spot is for me?"

My mother's dark green eyes, the ones that matched mine perfectly, narrowed while she thought. "You're different, Kate. You've always been easygoing, unemotional, basically difficult to read. I think he's spent his life understanding you."

The phone rang, announcing the beginning of another day of campaigning for my mother. A smile blossomed on her face with the greeting from the other end.

"Hi, Ron! I'm so glad you called me back. Joe and I had such a wonderful time at the fundraiser and it was great meeting Kitty. Your wife is amazing and what an incredible cook!" I glanced at my mother when she wasn't looking, while she was in full gushing mode. The difference, though, between her and most other adults was that it wasn't an act. Her genuine love of people was real and tangible, whether you were Ron, the wealthy lobbyist who could manipulate political parties, or Bill, the janitor at Disneyland, a man my mother had spent twenty minutes talking to during a summer vacation at the Magic Kingdom.

"I know the Democratic fundraiser is coming up, and I definitely want to pick your brain that night and get your advice. Your support would be so incredible for my campaign. Do you have a few minutes, because I did have some ideas for the fundraiser that might draw more people. Can you hang on for a moment?"

My mother covered the mouthpiece and turned to me. "Honey, are you okay, or do you need me to talk with you about this some more?"

I shook my head no and popped the last of my bagel in my mouth. She nodded in return and began plowing through her stack of files while she effusively detailed the creative ideas that would no doubt impress Ron.

I went on with my day but I found myself wondering what would have happened to our conversation had the phone not rung. Would the pleasant, relaxed words have incinerated into the ashes of bickering and disappointment? The kernel of normalcy I'd experienced with my mother for those few precious moments left me deeply sentimental for the past and the friendship we used to share—the relationship that was envied by all of my peers who told me they wished they could be in my family.

Later that night I curled up with my journal, quickly imprinting my ideas on three pages with no hesitancy of thought, no pausing for editing. My eyes glanced at my backpack, the pink withdrawal slip hanging from the front pocket, like a tongue stuck out, chiding me for my decision.

April 14, 1983

Dear Sis,

And they think Jimmy Carter had a tough time explaining HIS brother!
Well, what can I say? You must know how I feel about your decision.
Personally, I'm very proud of you, and no, I don't think I'm jumping the gun.
I'm being proud right now—before you take your first bribe.

I wonder if women politicians talk about taking their first bribe in
the same manner in which they express themselves about the first sexual
experience? Or as much?

Now just because I may find it expedient to make an occasional request
once my very own sister has established her political clout, it doesn't mean
for a second that I approve of nepotism. Nevertheless, I want you to keep the
following points of potential requests in the back of your mind:

1.Establishment of Artist in Residence program on all state and
community college campuses. Guaranteed state income of 52,000 per year or
the right to raise marijuana, whichever comes first.

2. *Immediate arrest and execution of one Nestor C. Porter should he fail to pay one Charles E. Driscoll all monies due within 24 hours of being warned by the above named party. Method of execution to be determined at the whim of any embittered, young Puerto Rican girl.*

Never mind my motives, just do it.

I'd offer you my talents, but I'm not sure what I could contribute. Maybe if you need someone to kick off a whisper campaign or design some slanderous posters. I do know a number of people who would kneecap your opponent, but they would want favors later on.

Have you given any thought to running under another name? Why not? I'm only thinking of your husband's good name. And what will happen to the children if you are caught in the middle of some unspeakable, sleazy political scandal? Don't let my innocent questions bother you. You will soon be subject to all sorts of embarrassing inquiries, such as:

Are you a communist?

Why not?

How did you vote in the Hayes/Tilden election?

Did you ever sleep with Richard Nixon?

Really?

That many times??!!??

Was he as good as they say?

Being from Missouri, have you ever been compromised?

My good friend Nestor has just vacated my apartment on the way to Poon, India, where he intends to hold a political rally in support of your candidacy. If we can raise the cash for boat fare, don't be surprised if a small delegation of lepers shows up at your next soiree.

I hope all is well, especially between you and Kate. My dear sister, if you can endure me, you can certainly accept your gay daughter.

Let the campaign begin!

Charles

Buddy Boy

For high school seniors, May is the cruelest month. In the minds of the near-graduates, school has really ended and this extra month is only added torture. Colleges have already given notice so grades don't matter, only graduation. Seniors spend their time sitting in classes thinking about how much money they'll make over the summer, who their college roommates will be and most of all, their major during college.

I had absolutely no idea. I'd thought about becoming an activist, spending my life going from town to town, marching, getting arrested and trying to put an end to homophobia everywhere. I'd made it out to be very glamorous but I didn't imagine it would be very prosperous and deep down I knew I was a capitalist at heart.

James, Beth and I had spent more than a few Friday nights discussing our futures at Buddy's, the local hangout for seniors smart enough not to party into a drunken stupor after the football games and yet cool enough to appreciate good coffee. I had seriously thought about attending a few of the most hedonistic beer busts where liquor and drugs were prevalent, clothing was optional and the police were called on a regular basis—just to see how my mother, the state senator and rising public figure, would react to her lesbian daughter in handcuffs. My good sense prevailed, especially since Beth promised me hot sex after our evenings at Buddy's concluded.

Buddy's was a Phoenix landmark. All of us remembered growing up with Buddy Burgers, a once-a-week staple in any Phoenician's diet. As kids, we loved the burgers, but we also loved Buddy, the huge ceramic statue of a boy dressed in blue overalls holding a Buddy Burger high in the air on a plate. Despite his height (ten feet from hamburger to toe), Buddy's cherubic face and sweeping blond hair made him an instant hit with any young child. Growing up didn't mean abandoning Buddy's. Instead of going for dinner with the folks, now we drove ourselves for late-night coffee.

We were regulars and good friends with Robin, the night manager. Beth and I both had a crush on her. We suspected she was a closeted dyke or a woman who just hadn't figured it all out yet. She loved James's biting humor, so she gave us free coffee and a booth next to the Buddy Boy.

"I can't believe we're about to graduate!" Beth exclaimed the Friday before the ceremony.

"Some of us may not," James said sadly. He hung his head and stirred his coffee.

"You are going to graduate," I replied firmly. "We studied all last weekend, James. I know you passed."

James gave a halfhearted smile and kissed me on the cheek.

I had been tutoring James all year in economics, a class he just couldn't grasp, perhaps because James had never worried about money. Fifty-dollar bills just magically appeared in his wallet each week, his allowance from his father, the owner of the most prominent construction company in Phoenix. James had no idea how money worked, except that he liked to spend it on himself and others.

"We need to stay on topic, people," Beth chided. "Our goal tonight is to think of the Senior Prank. We don't have a lot of time." Beth looked at me and I rolled my eyes.

"I don't know what to do," I said. "If we do anything fun, we're going to be in trouble. Principal Kellogg pulled me into his office yesterday. He reminded me that there can't be a repeat of last year and whatever we do, it better not be excessive."

The year before, fifty live rats had been freed on the dais during the graduation ceremony, causing the superintendent to jump, fall off the platform and sustain a fractured wrist.

"What does Principal Kellogg consider *excessive*?" James asked slyly.

"A single water balloon is too much," Beth retorted. She took my hand underneath the booth and caressed my fingers. We needed to make a decision fast, so Beth and I could ditch James and retreat to our latest sex lair, an apartment belonging to Beth's brother.

I ignored Beth's growing passion and focused on James. "All I know is that if there's anything over the top, we're not getting our diplomas."

"The key," James said, holding his spoon up for emphasis, "is to make Principal Kellogg laugh. If we plan something clever, and he thinks it's funny, he probably won't suspend us and he'll let us march with the class."

Beth and I nodded our heads in agreement.

"So what do we do?" I asked quickly. Beth had moved close to me and was massaging my thigh lightly.

Different ideas ran through my head but none was appropriate. I was too distracted by Beth's touch. We sat there for a while, watching the general commotion around us. James nodded at a group of our peers seated across from us. I glanced through the cheap window blinds at a car full of giggling juniors, just sitting in the parking lot trying to look cool for the senior boys who cruised up and down Central Avenue.

"You know, when I move to San Francisco in the fall, I'm going to miss Buddy," James said absently, the prank momentarily forgotten.

We all looked at Buddy, his broad smile staring down at us.

"I know what you mean," Beth added.

"Maybe we could take Buddy with us," I joked.

"Are you kidding?" Beth exclaimed. "That statue's gotta weigh a thousand pounds."

"No," James disagreed, "it's probably only a couple hundred. It wouldn't be that hard to move."

Beth's hand was clearly in control of my body and I decided I could care less about a senior prank. We could be remembered as the mature class of the Eighties. Nobody would need to know that the senior class vice president of 1983 was too much in lust with her girlfriend to bother with it.

"I want you," I whispered in her ear.

James cleared his throat to get our attention. We were being rude and he found it amusing. "Ladies, as much as I enjoy watching you make a scene, we have some planning to do." His eyes danced with excitement. "I have an idea. Our friend Buddy is going to do some traveling."

James would never have taken Buddy without asking Robin's permission. When she found out what James wanted to do, she was flattered that we wanted to include the Buddy Boy in our senior prank and more than anything else, she saw the opportunity for some free publicity.

James made a few phone calls and an hour after Buddy's closed, four of his father's burly construction employees appeared and helped James load Buddy into a flatbed. I looked around and saw no one I knew, particularly Principal Kellogg. I imagined his yellow Pinto squealing into the parking lot, his headlights spotlighting our criminal activity.

"Where are you going to put him?" Robin asked before we drove away.

James laughed. "You'll see. Honey, *you will see*." Beth and I started to howl because we knew Buddy's destination—the top of the school auditorium.

Getting Buddy on top of the auditorium wasn't easy. James had borrowed several ropes and pulleys from his father's business and it took all of us working together to pull him up the side of the large building. We were ready to collapse by the time we positioned Buddy at the furthest corner of the auditorium, his chunky silhouette and hamburger shining in the moonlight.

"Doesn't he look great?" James cried with joy. He was jumping up and down like a child. James beamed with pride at having thought of a truly hilarious but nonviolent act to perpetrate on the school. This certainly was more creative than the rats of '81, the goat blood of '80 and the class of '79's Volkswagen Beetle prank in the principal's office.

"Buddy's never looked better," I agreed.

At six the next morning I awoke to a DJ laughing hysterically about Valley High's extraordinary senior prank. When Beth, James and I got to school, most of the students were standing on the auditorium steps, mesmerized at the sight of Buddy. Also present was Principal Kellogg, walkie-talkie in hand, trying to act like he knew what to do about the giant hamburger boy sitting on the rooftop. He would talk into the radio, look up at Buddy, scratch his head and listen to whomever he was speaking. The bell rang and nobody moved. Principal Kellogg made a feeble attempt to move people toward their classes but everyone wanted to see how the "Buddy Incident" would be resolved.

A group of janitors approached with some heavy ropes and hooks. They were going to try to lower Buddy from the roof.

"They shouldn't do that," James said, shaking his head. "He'll never make it."

Beth took James's arm. "James, you'd better go talk to Principal Kellogg. If anything happens to Buddy, Robin will be really pissed."

James saw the dilemma. If he advised Principal Kellogg, he could be giving himself away, but still, he had promised Robin that Buddy would be safe.

The three of us approached Principal Kellogg who was still mumbling into the walkie-talkie, apparently to the superintendent.

"Principal Kellogg," James interrupted, "I think you'd better let me get Buddy off the roof."

Principal Kellogg turned off the walkie-talkie. "Do you know something about this James?"

James shuddered. "Me? No, Sir. But my father's in the construction business and I know you'll need some different equipment to get Buddy down."

Most of the students had gathered around us and Principal Kellogg was well aware that he was on display to most of the student body.

"What about you, Kate? Can you tell me who put Buddy on the roof?"

"I don't know," I said, not sounding convincing to anyone, even myself.

"Well, if that's the case, then you're the first vice president who didn't participate in the senior prank."

"HEADS UP!" cried several loud voices in unison.

We turned to see Buddy sailing toward the ground. During the confrontation with Principal Kellogg, we'd forgotten about the over-zealous janitors who'd ascended the ladders and tried to bring the Buddy Boy down. We watched as Buddy turned over in a perfect front flip and landed on his extended burger arm. The burger exploded and a cloud of ceramic dust choked us all.

We ran to Buddy. He lay on his side, his burger arm destroyed and the right side of his face shattered. We could see into the hollow body, full of chicken wire and splintered wood. Buddy was gone.

Realizing I was his best possible source of information and wanting to fight on his own turf, Principal Kellogg summoned me to his office. I followed a step behind him all the way to the administration building, trying to think of what I would say. The previous vice president had told me to play dumb, because Principal Kellogg really couldn't do anything without evidence. Since we hadn't been caught on the roof at one in the morning and I was pretty sure there were no witnesses, it would just be his accusation against my denial.

I took the only chair in his office while he paced behind his vast expanse of a desk.

"Kate, I'm going to come right to the point. I believe this prank is excessive and a disruption to the flow of the educational system and it will not be tolerated." Principal Kellogg sat down while I digested his sentence.

"But I don't know anything," I insisted.

"Bullshit," he said quietly. "Miss Mitchell, I want you in my office tomorrow afternoon at three o' clock with the names of the perpetrators of this prank. If you maintain this ridiculous silence, then you, young lady, will not be marching at graduation."

"You can't do that!"

Principal Kellogg grinned. "I most certainly can. After last year's fiasco with the rats, the superintendent has given me free reign to deal with pranks that are hazardous to our students. And certainly, having a two-ton statue fly off the auditorium and nearly crash into innocent bystanders qualifies as hazardous. If you want to march, I suggest you start talking." He picked up the phone and began dialing to signal the end of our conversation.

When I arrived home that afternoon, both of my parents were waiting for me, as well as my grandmother, who just wanted to know the gossip. Apparently the phone had rung nonstop, reporters wanting to talk to me and my mother. After the tenth call, my father finally unplugged it.

"Kate, you don't have a choice. You need to tell the principal who was involved," my mother insisted.

I kicked at the carpet with my sandal, unable to look at my parents. My relationship with my mother had improved, mainly because she was always engaged in civil servant events, making the state of Arizona a better place and avoiding her lesbian daughter.

My father sat down next to me on the sofa and put his arm around me. He and I had grown closer during the past year as he asked more questions rather than casting judgments about my lifestyle. "Kate, honey, I'm going to guess that you were involved, simply because you're the vice president and we've had about thirty phone calls in the last two weeks asking about the senior prank. So, I'm assuming you know about it. But if other people helped, then they should suffer the consequences too."

"Ah hell, Joe," my grandmother disagreed. "Kate isn't a snitch, are you, Kate?"

My grandmother winked at me and I smiled. "Besides," she continued, "that principal is an ass."

"Mom!" my mother cried.

"Jiminy, Barbara! That was the funniest thing I've ever seen! That big fat statue, with his burger waving in the air, damndest funniest sight . . ." She started to laugh, and then I laughed. My father joined us and the three of us laughed so hard we cried, until Grandma's dentures fell out and sent us into another spasm of laughter.

Only my mother remained stoic, tapping her foot, waiting. "I do not find this funny," she said icily. "Kate isn't going to participate in her own graduation and I don't think that's fair, since I know she couldn't put that statue up there on her own." We wiped our eyes and took a breath, knowing my mother wasn't done. "Can I assume that Beth was involved?" I shrugged, but she didn't notice. "Of course she was. You two are inseparable."

"Dammit, Mom!" I exploded. "Don't go there. That's not what this conversation is about."

"Of course it is, Kate! You try to impress her with everything you do and she's not a good influence."

"Let's talk about what you're really concerned about, which is the voters and the fact that all of the newspapers tomorrow morning will have a picture of the Valley High Senior Prank on the front page, wondering which seniors participated. And if I'm the only one who gets in trouble, then that really looks bad for you, doesn't it?"

My mother shook her head and smoothed her skirt. "My position has nothing to do with this," she said softly.

"Of course it does. I'm a reflection of you." I nearly spat the words out, knowing they would appall and disgust her.

For the first time in nearly two months, my mother met my eyes, her face intolerant, and her lips bent into a smirk. "I certainly hope not," she snapped back.

"We're done," I announced, retreating to my bedroom.

I spent most of the evening on the phone with my friends, all of whom had advice. As I hung up from talking to Beth, the phone immediately rang again. It was James.

"Have you heard?" I asked James.

"Who hasn't?"

"Where have you been? I tried to call you earlier."

"I was out to dinner with my folks," James said excitedly. "Kate, you're not going to believe it! I passed my economics final!"

I couldn't help but smile. "That's great, James. You worked really hard."

"Hey, Kate," James said softly, "What are you going to tell Principal K tomorrow?"

"Nothing."

"Maybe you should tell him the truth," James offered.

"Nah," I sighed, wiping away a tear I was glad he couldn't see. "If I tell him, then all those study nights will go to waste."

He laughed slightly. "Thanks, sweetie. Hey," he quickly added, "I'm going to think of something, okay?"

"Yeah," I said, although the tears were streaming down my face.

By the following afternoon I was distressed. During the school day I received support from friends, teachers and even the vice principal, who cautioned me that Principal Kellogg meant business. The rat incident had pushed the superintendent over the edge.

When I arrived at the principal's office promptly at three o'clock, he was in an unscheduled meeting. I waited and waited. I didn't really need any more time to ponder and possibly change the decision I'd reached during my last period class. We'd been reading Thoreau in senior English and the whole notion of nonviolent civil disobedience touched a nerve. At four I was about to leave, when the principal's door burst open and a man I vaguely recognized stormed past me. James emerged, a smile on his face, and I realized the irate adult was James's father, Irvin Moore. James winked at me and caught up to his father. Principal Kellogg leaned against the door frame, loosening his tie. Sweat poured down his sideburns and he was dabbing his forehead with a handkerchief. Either the air conditioning was down or Mr. Moore had gained control of Principal Kellogg's internal thermostat.

He looked at my bewildered face and blushed. "Kate, in regard to that little matter we discussed yesterday . . ." His voice trailed off as he grabbed the doorknob. "Please consider it closed," he murmured, before slamming the door shut.

James was leaning against my car when I returned to the parking lot, dazed by the entire incident, unable to believe that I would get to march with my class.

"What the hell happened, James?"

James casually polished his sunglasses with his shirt, not answering until they shaded his eyes again. "Sometimes, honey, it pays to have money." He said it as a little rhyme, and started laughing at his own humor.

"Your dad bribed Principal Kellogg?"

"Yeah, in a way, I guess he did. My father just reminded Mr. K. that Moore Construction was building the new gymnasium next year at a substantially lower rate and if that deal fell through, the superintendent might not be very happy."

I nodded. "But why'd your father help me out, James? He hardly knows me!"

James leaned forward and took my hand. "Katie, my dad owed

you."

"Owed me? For what?"

"For getting me through high school! You're the reason I'm graduating and my dad knows that."

"James, it's not like I pulled you from a burning building. I just tutored you in economics." Although I appreciated James's gratitude, the fact was, James's scholastic problems were all psychological.

James kissed me on the cheek.

"What was that for?"

"For being the best teacher I've had all year."

"C'mon, James, that's silly."

"No, Kate, I'm serious. You should have been the one collecting the paycheck. You're better at explaining things than most of those lazy old farts!" He kissed me again before bounding away. When he got to his own car, he turned and emoted in full dramatic voice, "You, my friend, are a teacher!"

April 22, 1985

Sis,

All goes well in Tucson. Spring has come full bloom and the weather is appropriately quasi-sexual. What time I am not obliged to spend in the pursuit of filthy lucre working as a drug counselor, I spend with my children. Except for them and a few friends, I have become a virtual recluse. Sizemore, one of the more deliciously demented individuals with whom I deal daily at the hospital, has told me that becoming a recluse is actually a good thing. He lived in his mother's linen closet for six years. He should know. But unlike Sizemore, I think I accomplish a trifle more than he.

It's hard to believe I've reached the big 4-0! I have noticed I have become downright stingy with my time. My son takes a great deal of it, but with him it's more like an act of rejuvenation. But other people are becoming a polyglot of energy devouring rhetoricians for whom I have little time and no answers. Had I known that turning forty permits one to grow so delightfully cranky, I would have aged more a long time ago.

My dear son Phineus gave me a poem—it went:
"Are I People?
No, you are chicken.
Do chickens come from people?
No, chickens come from eggs.
Are eggs born?
No, eggs are laid.
Are people laid?
Not all, some are chicken."
I'm going to have to have a talk with that boy. He's not getting any younger, either.

Mysteriously I find some time to sit around and write. Phineus is in the other room trying to figure out some of the passages in a Harold Robbins novel, and I am helping an illegal alien named Oscar with his junior college lit course. He wants to be a computer analyst, assuming immigration doesn't interfere. Tonight we are writing a paper on James Joyce, or as Oscar says, Hames Hoyce. It is titled, "Target: Finnegan's Wake: What the Shit!"

I've got to go. Phineus is asking me to define venereal . . .
My deepest love and affection,
Charles

Present Day

Thunder bellows in the distance, announcing the arrival of the rain that has just passed Central Phoenix and is headed for the east valley. The charcoal sky brings gentler temperatures and light beads of water dust the ground. Fortunately the monsoon did not pour buckets, allowing us to stay on schedule and keep a promise I'd made to my mother a week before.

I pull through the gates of the cemetery, noting the appropriateness of the dark sky over the headstones and graves, like a cloak shielding the lost souls from the harsh Phoenix summer and blinding sunlight. My mother will benefit from the weather today and it will not dictate the length of her visit. She can enjoy life on her own timetable without my father and me nagging her about the effects of the heat.

My parents are already at the crest of the hill and my father has managed to situate my mother in her wheelchair. I curse under my breath in private, rather than berating my father publicly for moving my mother without help. They are waiting for me, my father squatting beside my mother, patting her hand, talking to her as he has for the last forty-one years, undeterred by her lack of responsiveness or participation in the conversation. I realize that since my mother's illness and for the first time in their marriage, it is my father's voice and his opinions that dominate conversations.

I pull up behind the Buick and wave as I get out. A light breeze passes and I inhale deeply, enjoying the smell of rain on the fresh cut grass. I notice my mother holds a bouquet of lilies, my grandmother's favorite flower, and I wonder if she has remembered this trivial fact or if my father thought to purchase them on his own.

"Hi Mom. How's it going today?"

"It's going well. How are you?"

"I'm fine. Sarah and Luke are in Wisconsin visiting her folks."

"How's her folks?" my mother thinks to ask.

"They're fine." I search for another topic quickly, not wishing to dwell on the subject of Sarah's parents, who are ten years older than mine, enjoying their retirement with travel and friends, living the American Dream with the RV and the freedom to go, while my parents remain shackled by the chains of my mother's disease.

I lean over and kiss her cheek, avoiding the bright red lipstick painted on her face. "It's beautiful today, don't you think?"

"Actually, I'm a little warm."

With my mother's pronouncement, my father works to remove the light sweater that covers her blouse. It's not unusual for my mother to be hot. Even in a polar freeze, she would probably still be sweating. When the sweater is discarded to the backseat of the car, we start the descent down the cement path, counting rows as we go. We have not been here in a year, and all of the grave markers look exactly the same.

"Yes, it's pretty warm today," my mother continues, as my father and I whisper, trying to get our bearings and determine which row holds my grandparents' graves.

"I think it's the next one," my father comments. "I think we're too far west."

I shake my head, unsure. Every plot looks the same to me, the tract house version of the afterlife, and yet another reason why I will choose cremation, as my uncle did. We will most likely need a map to locate my grandparents' double marker and I turn to tell my father that I'm going back to the office.

"This is the right row," my mother states. She points her finger to the left. "Mom and Dad are over there."

I walk through the wet grass, following my mother's directions, glancing at the names rising from the ground. Sure enough, halfway down the line is Driscoll. I have to chuckle and shrug my shoulders at her certainty and accuracy. I return to my place behind her chair and guide her through the soft ground, the wheels sinking in the rain-soaked grass. I am sweating slightly from the workout and the bottoms of my shoes are covered in mud by the time I've pushed her to my grandparents. My father takes the lilies from her hand and gently places them between the bronze markers.

"No, don't put them there," Mom scolds. "Dad hated lilies. Just put them on Mom's."

My father obliges and we stand in silence, honoring my grandparents. I watch her face, concerned at her reaction, waiting for possible tears or anger, but none come. Instead she sits stone-faced, aware of the solemnity of the moment but perhaps without recognition. Just the day before at the care center, she had told me her mother was upstairs and she was meeting her for lunch. How much my mother understands now, hovering over her own mother's grave, I don't know and her expressions reveal nothing.

I wonder if her mind drifts to the memories, as mine does, or if she is unable to string together the laughter, the fights and the endless flurry of activity that defined my grandmother throughout her life. I touch my mother gently on the shoulder as if the physical connection allows her to partake in my remembrances of my grandmother, who was by far a much better grandparent than she was a mother.

I glance at the sky, the dark grays drifting to the east while a palette of blues remain overhead. I know my mother will wish to stay here for as long as we allow and I have my own agenda today.

"I'll be back in a bit, Mom," I say.

"Are you leaving?" she asks, a bit hurt.

"Oh, no. I'm just going to see another friend. I'll be back. I'm not going away."

Reassured, she smiles and returns to face my grandparents. My father nods at me. He knows the significance of today and I haven't even reminded him. Our relationship has developed over the years into quiet respect borne from love and words are unnecessary to understand our hearts' motivations.

I return to the crest of the hill and my eyes travel the expanse of the cemetery in all different directions, searching, looking for what is the compass to my past. I squint, unused to the dreary landscape that increases my nearsightedness. Eventually I find the peak of the monolith in the distance and begin my trek toward it, passing around hundreds of markers, the mausoleum and a giant fountain that sits in the middle of an exclusive, private garden for the wealthy who can afford to be buried in the Serenity Cascades area. I've made this walk many times before, journeying between my grandmother's grave to the monolith, the distance of which I decided long ago is symbolic of the worst year of my life, my freshman year in college.

The year had begun with great expectation, my grandmother agreeing to finance my education at Oberlin, much to my mother's emphatic displeasure. By October, though, Grandma was on her deathbed and while her dying wish to my mother was that I would graduate from Oberlin, she couldn't foresee the grief that lay ahead or my mother's vengeful determination to make me want to leave the school on my own. She had been beaten, my father siding with my grandmother, but she wouldn't accept it gracefully.

Feelings of abandonment overwhelmed me as I made the huge leap into adulthood and I would never forget my father pulling away from my dormitory after I'd moved in, my mother refusing to accompany us to Ohio. I had voluntarily plunged into an environment where I knew no one and my ties to my roots had withered. Beth and James had moved away, finding their own lives, my grandmother was dead, my father was not one to communicate frequently from a distance and my mother said nothing, except when my father handed her the phone for our routine Sunday night call. She sent no letters, initiated no phone calls and showed no interest in my success, or rather, growing failure in college. My familial despair translated to poor social skills and I made few friends initially, the hours outside of class spent studying in the library or reading on my small, twin bed that faced the center of campus.

I close my eyes and see the drab, tan paint, its sheen gone long before I arrived. The square room became my haven and my prison simultaneously, and decades later, when I first entered my mother's room at Dayport Care Center, I recognized the uncanny similarity in the two living spaces.

I stop at the top of the next hill and gaze toward the easternmost section of the cemetery, hunting for the ivory point that is my destination. It is sandwiched between cement statues and enormous crosses made in homage to loved ones who could afford much more than a simple brass marker. I keep my eyes focused on the monolith as I start through the grass again, ignoring the cement paths that create a more circuitous route than I wish to take. I am halfway to the monolith now and in the story of my freshman year, at the end of the first semester, tainted by my uncle's sudden death one afternoon in his backyard. He collapsed and never awoke, never gave any of us the chance to say good-bye. His desire to be cremated created a firestorm between my mother and his ex-wife, who wished to honor his request. I sided with my aunt, creating yet another point of friction with my mother and a guarantee that she would ignore my existence for a great while longer.

I dreaded returning to school for the second semester but my mother's cold indifference drove me back to the snowy Ohio winter and the four walls of my dormitory room. Over the holiday break I had inherited a roommate, a vibrant rebel named Mason, who wore only black, her dark hair streaked with shocking bleach-white strands. People turned their head when she passed by, perhaps because of her hair or clothes or most likely because her nose and eyebrow were pierced.

"I learned everything I need to know about hair and dress from the Sex Pistols," she told me.

We became friends because I found her intriguing, and frankly, because I had no one else. Initially Mason thought she was living with a prude. My side of the room reeked of traditional upbringing, with displayed family photos, a few stuffed animals resting on the flowered comforter of my bed, electric typewriter perched on my desk next to my schoolbooks and preppie clothes neatly folded in the standard issue dorm dresser.

Mason had converted her half of the room into night, and since she had the windows on her side, which she painted black along with most everything else, the entire room was transformed into negative energy. She'd overturned her dresser on the floor and draped a black sheet over it, placing her prized possession in the center—a large bong. The dresser drawers were haphazardly stacked in the corner, filled with black jeans and concert T-shirts, the only apparel Mason ever wore. Her black leather jacket hung on the chair that sat under the unused desk for Mason rarely went to class and never purchased textbooks. Most prominent was her collection of beer bottles from around the world, which she proudly displayed along the window ledge.

Over the next few months, her lifestyle encroached upon mine. Her personality was magnetic and she attracted all kinds of people who reveled in her difference, since most of them didn't have the courage of a nonconformist but respected Mason for hers. While I was hesitant of Mason's lifestyle and felt ignorant of life in her presence, I felt disconnected from everyone and everything I had known. Family, which had once been the core of my being, now sat at the periphery, irrelevant in the decisions I made. The interactions I was forced to have with them were a chore and done only to keep my father's financial lifeline flowing. To my mother, I was the proverbial black sheep and she was grateful that thousands of miles separated me from her ever-growing political career. There were rumors she would run for a top state seat in government and if that did indeed occur, I was sure she would happily finance my graduate level education—as long as it was on another continent.

My family was distant in every sense of the word but Mason was only across the room. Time was irrelevant to her and seven in the morning was as good a time as any to start a party. People were constantly in our room at all hours and the smell of marijuana never faded. Within two months of Mason's arrival, my typewriter disappeared under an avalanche of all-black second-hand clothes I'd purchased at a thrift store, I was eating Cheerios and drinking beer for breakfast, most of my spending money was going up in literal smoke and I no longer shared my bed with stuffed animals, but women of all shapes and sizes. Days and weeks were spent in a drunken and/or drugged-out stupor and when my father called after receiving my midterms (I was failing everything), I couldn't even hold a coherent conversation, my mind blinded by my first acid trip.

When he appeared in my room a few days later, his eyes welled up with tears at the sight of me. I opened the door, expecting anyone but him, wearing only black bikini briefs and a skimpy undershirt that hid nothing. I hadn't slept for two days and my eyes were dull and red from the drugs I'd enjoyed throughout the weekend.

He looked past me to my bed, at the naked blonde toking up on a joint we had just rolled. The acrid smell of weed drifted into the hallway and my father's senses were violated.

"Get your things, Kate. We're leaving."

"What?" I cried.

"You're done. I've already spoken to the dean and the dorm supervisor. I'm taking you home today. Now." His voice was firm and there was no negotiation. I was packed in less than an hour and the trip back to the Southwest was a blur of humiliation, my father and I only exchanging words when it was absolutely necessary. He didn't really take me home but instead to Tucson, to a rehabilitation center for drug addiction. He assured me that the reason I went to Tucson and not to Phoenix had nothing to do with my mother's political career.

It was probably the only lie my father ever told me.

The monolith towers over the other tributes to the dead, casting a prominent shadow, marking its power, stating its importance. I sit on the bench in front of it and I can't help but read the gold plaque at its base, although I have the words committed to memory.

James Augustus Moore
Beloved Brother and Friend
1964-1983

My good friend James, the person responsible for planting the seeds of my career, the boy who seemed to have the world at his disposal, led a charade of a life. He had indeed moved to San Francisco as a lustful youth and enrolled in a few classes at Golden Gate University to make his father happy. Most of his time, though, was spent in the bathhouses and the apartments of older men. While James was truly the air of life, he wasn't smart and he became HIV-positive before I left Oberlin. When he called with his shattering news, I couldn't even process the implications since I was numb to everything except drugs and alcohol.

We didn't speak after that fragmented phone call but I looked forward to seeing him and explaining my thoughtlessness once I'd been discharged from rehab. I saw James and me as parallel lines, both of us reaping the consequences of choices. Our meeting never happened, as he committed suicide two days before I came home. He'd been forced to come out to his father in order to begin his HIV treatment but instead of compassion and sympathy, James's father showed only heartlessness, disowning him and forbidding him from ever stepping foot in the house again. James was dead the next day, found hanging from a steel beam at one of his father's job sites. He'd hung himself with a length of rope, adeptly tying the noose he'd learned years before in Boy Scouts.

His father refused to bury him, so his eldest brother agreed to pay for James's funeral and erect a tribute in his brother's name. His choice of a phallic symbol was no accident and a final slap in their father's face. Oddly, it was James's death that helped me crawl out of my black hole, return to college at the University of Arizona and meet Sarah, my savior. She was the one who bridged the gap between my mother and me.

I close my eyes, feeling the tears coming, grateful that I only visit the cemetery once a year, on the anniversary of James's death. The memories that are rekindled each time are the same, for they have taken root in my mind. No new visions emerge and it is the sharpest points of the story that stay with me each year as I make the long walk from my grandmother to James, with thoughts of my uncle interspersed.

My cell phone chirps, and I thrust my hand into my purse quickly, thinking it might be Luke or Sarah.

"Hello?"

"Hey. Are you sitting with James?"

I smile at the sound of Beth's voice. "Yes, I'm here. How did you know?"

She giggles just the way she did as a teenager. "Oh, a little bird told me."

"Sarah," I conclude.

"Uh-huh. She called me last night and said I had to call this morning because she was worried about you."

"I don't know why she'd be worried. I do this every year."

"C'mon, sweetie. This year's a little different. You know, with your mom getting sick and none of us there. I think she had reason to be concerned."

"Well, I'm fine. It's always hard being here, and all the memories that come back."

"I know," she says quietly. "But hey, some of those memories were pretty awesome. We had great times together, right?"

I smile, and the image of the Buddy Boy skips through my mind. "Yeah," I agree. "Where are you?"

"I'm on location in Bermuda right now. You should feel really honored. The whole production is being held up so I can talk to you."

"Oh, God. I am flattered. But don't let me keep you. Are you and Kristin coming to Phoenix for Christmas?"

"Yup. And we might have some big news."

"Is she pregnant?" I ask excitedly.

Beth laughs gleefully. "Not yet but she's really applying the pressure. We've got to live up to you and Sarah. You're our role models, you know."

"Yeah, right."

Beth sighs deeply. "I've got to go. Say a prayer to James, tell your parents hi for me, kiss Sarah and give Luke a big hug from his Aunt Beth."

"I will."

"You know how much I love you, don't you, Katie? Always and forever, right?"

I'm crying again, only now it's the tears of the fresh rain and I am rejuvenated. "I know. I love you, too. I'll see you soon."

I do say a prayer to James and trek back to the car where my parents are waiting for me.

"I'll need to bring the dogs in," my mother comments as she looks to the sky. I'm not sure she realizes I've been gone for the better part of an hour.

"Where's Sarah?" she asks.

"She's with Luke in Wisconsin, Mom."

"Oh, that's right," she says, remembering that I'd told her that before.

I push her chair to the car door and open it. "We took Luke to the ocean last week. I'll have him bring the pictures next time he visits."

"Oh I'd love to see them!" she exclaims.

"Yes, he looks pretty happy. He loves the ocean."

"Oh, I know he does. He's a real . . . a real . . . ocean lover."

My father and I settle my mother, her oxygen and the wheelchair into the car, much like a pit crew at the Indy 500. Certain things must be done in a precise order and way and time is critical, since my mother and her breathing tube cannot be separated for long.

I hug my father as he moves to the driver's side and I return to my mother. When I kneel down to kiss her good-bye, she taps my cheek gently with her fingertips.

"I really like you."

"I like you too, Mom," I reply.

Sensing I'm patronizing her, she repeats herself. "No, I really like you. You're a terrific mom. You're great."

Her sentiment has broken through the walls of her disease and she is absolutely certain of her emotions and the genuine feeling touches my heart. "Well," I respond, "I had a lot of help. You're a great mom, too."

"You try so hard," she says. "You try so hard. You really do. I really admire you."

I kiss her cheek, grateful for these slices of reality. "Thanks Mom. I'll be by to see you tomorrow."

She furrows her brow in worry. "I'm not sure where I'll be. I've got a lot to do tomorrow. I've got a meeting and a whole lot of people to call."

I smile and will myself not to cry. "I'll find you," I say. "I'll find you."

Publications from Spinsters Ink

P.O. Box 242
Midway, Florida 32343
Phone: 800 301-6860
www.spinstersink.com

DISORDERLY ATTACHMENTS by Jennifer L. Jordan. 5th Kristin Ashe Mystery. Kris investigates whether a mansion someone wants to convert into condos is haunted.   ISBN 1-883523-74-5 $14.95

VERA'S STILL POINT by Ruth Perkinson. Vera is reminded of exactly what it is that she has been missing in life.
                            ISBN 1-883523-73-7 $14.95

OUTRAGEOUS by Sheila Ortiz-Taylor. Arden Benbow, a motor-cycle riding, lesbian Latina poet from LA is hired to teach poetry in a small liberal arts college in northwest Florida.
                            ISBN 1-883523-72-9 $14.95

UNBREAKABLE by Blayne Cooper. The bonds of love and friend-ship can be as strong as steel. But are they unbreakable?
                            ISBN 1-883523-76-1 $14.95

ALL BETS OFF by Jaime Clevenger. Bette Lawrence is about to find out how hard life can be for someone of low society standing in the 1900s.   ISBN 1-883523-71-0 $14.95

UNBEARABLE LOSSES by Jennifer L. Jordan. 4th in the Kristin Ashe Mystery series. Two elderly sisters have hired Kris to discover who is pilfering from their award-winning holiday display.
                            ISBN 1-883523-68-0 $14.95

FRENCH POSTCARDS by Jane Merchant. When Elinor moves to France with her husband and two children, she never expects that her life is about to be changed forever.

ISBN 1-883523-67-2 $14.95

EXISTING SOLUTIONS by Jennifer L. Jordan. 2nd book in the Kristin Ashe Mystery series. When Kris is hired to find an activist's biological father, things get complicated when she finds herself falling for her client.

ISBN 1-883523-69-9 $14.95

A SAFE PLACE TO SLEEP by Jennifer L. Jordan. 1st in the Kristin Ashe Mystery series. Kris is approached by well-known lesbian Destiny Greaves with an unusual request. One that will lead Kris to hunt for her own missing childhood pieces.

ISBN 1-883523-70-2 $14.95

THE SECRET KEEPING by Francine Saint Marie. The Secret Keeping is a high stakes, girl-gets-girl romance, where the moral of the story is that money can buy you love if it's invested wisely.

ISBN: 1-883523-77-X $14.95

WOMEN'S STUDIES by Julia Watts. With humor and heart, Women's Studies follows one school year in the lives of these three young women and shows that in college, one's extracurricular activities are often much more educational than what goes on in the classroom.

ISBN: 1-883523-75-3 $14.95

A POEM FOR WHAT'S HER NAME by Dani O'Connor. Professor Dani O'Connor had pretty much resigned herself to the fact that there was no such thing as a complete woman. Then out of nowhere, along comes a woman who blows Dani's theory right out of the water.

ISBN: 1-883523-78-8 $14.95

Visit

Spinsters Ink

at

SpinstersInk.com

or call our toll-free number

1-800-301-6860